CW00553641

# A PARTY
# TO
# MURDER

*by*
## Marcia Kash
*and*
## Douglas E. Hughes

## SAMUEL FRENCH, INC.

45 WEST 25TH STREET     NEW YORK 10010
7623 SUNSET BOULEVARD HOLLYWOOD 90046
LONDON                    TORONTO

ISBN 0 573 62675 8          Printed in U.S.A.          # 18975

## IMPORTANT BILLING AND CREDIT REQUIREMENTS

A PARTY TO MURDER was first produced at Kawartha Summer Theatre, Canada in August 1996. It was subsequently produced at Ensemble Theatre in Cincinnati in September 1996 with the following cast:

REV. MERRYWEATHER / ELWOOD . . . . . . . . . . . . Gordon Greene

MRS. McKNIGHT / VALERIE . . . . . . . . . . . . . . . . . . . . Marcia Kash

KONRAD / CHARLES . . . . . . . . . . . . . . . . . . . . . . . . . . . . . Scott New

O'KARMA / HENRI . . . . . . . . . . . . . . . . . . . . . . . . . . . . . Regina Pugh

ERNIE / WILLY . . . . . . . . . . . . . . . . . . . . . . . . . . . . . . . Robert B. Rais

EVELYN / McKENZIE . . . . . . . . . . . . . . . . . . . . . . . . . . . Berni Weber

*Directed by*  Ron Ulrich

*Scenic Designer*  Kevin J. Murphy
*Costume Designer*  Gretchen Sears
*Lighting Designer*  Jay Depenbrock
*Stage Manager*  Amy Lewis

# CAST OF CHARACTERS:

**KONRAD / CHARLES:**
A successful mystery-novelist. English. Urbane, intelligent, well bred. The ultimate host.

**ERNIE / WILLY:**
Former football player, big, friendly, gregarious, good sense of humor. Around 40.

**EVELYN / McKENZIE:**
Fashion model, late twenties, witty, extroverted, a tough exterior. She is Elwood's girlfriend.

**MRS. McKNIGHT / VALERIE:**
Early to mid forties. Henri's older sister. Smart, savvy. Used to getting her own way. Very well turned out.

**O'KARMA / HENRI:** *(pronounced "Henry")*
Late twenties. Valerie's younger sister. Shy, easily intimidated. Dresses conservatively.

**FATHER GERRY MERRYWEATHER / ELWOOD:**
Mid-fifties, balding. Corporate CEO type. Confident, friendly. Powerful and he knows it.

## TIME:  Present

## PLACE:
A cottage on an Island, in the middle of a lake, somewhere in North America.

## ACT I

### *Scene One*

*(Setting: The living area of an older, rustic house on a tiny island in the middle of a lake. SL is a fireplace, above which hangs a portrait of Agatha Christie. US is a large bookcase filled with books. In the USR corner is an archway leading to the bathroom and bedroom off. The main door is on the upstage wall to the L of the bookcase. DSR is a large window with a practical window seat underneath, upon which sits a jack-o-lantern with a light burning in it. USL is a staircase leading off to the bedrooms. There is a love seat and an armchair facing the fireplace, in which a fire glows. This, apart from the jack-o-lantern, is the only source of light in the room. It is Halloween night. At rise, there is a table center stage. Around the table are seated KONRAD LEIMGRUBER, a suave, well-bred surgeon in his forties; EVELYN WATERS, a conservative-looking woman in her thirties; FATHER GERALD MERRIWEATHER, a priest in his fifties or sixties; MADAME O'KARMA, an exotic woman wearing a turban. In front of her is a crystal ball. Sitting at the head of the table with his face in a bowl of soup is ERNIE FENTON, a bald-headed man in his seventies. He appears to be dead. Spooky organ music plays underneath the following scene. Standing next to KONRAD is MRS. McKNIGHT, a maid. She is pointing a gun at KONRAD. Everyone stares at her.)*

MRS. McKNIGHT. I hate to do this, Sir.

KONRAD. Oh, just get on with it, Woman!

MRS. McKNIGHT. *(Deadpan)* If you insist, sir. *(She pulls the trigger on the gun, and a small flame shoots out the end. KONRAD holds up a cigar and puffs on it until it's lit.)* You must give those up, Dr. Leimgruber, sir. They're bad for your health.

KONRAD. Thank you for your concern, Mrs. McKnight. That will be all.

MRS. McKNIGHT. *(Indicating ERNIE.)* Is Mr. Fenton finished with his soup, sir?

KONRAD. That will be all. Thank you.

*(She curtsies perfunctorily, and begins to shuffle off L.)*

MADAME O'KARMA. No please don't go. I need everyone here.

MRS. McKNIGHT. *(To KONRAD.)* With your permission, sir.

KONRAD. Oh, very well.

*(KONRAD pulls up another chair and MRS. McKNIGHT joins the others at the table.)*

MADAME O'KARMA. Now, if I may have your attention, everyone. Please join hands, and concentrate ...

FATHER GERALD. This is a lot of superstitious nonsense. I could be defrocked just for being here.

EVELYN. And if the press ever finds out I am involved in a scandal like this, I can forget about getting re-elected.

O'KARMA. Father Gerald, Ms. Waters, please. I require your full attention.

EVELYN. Couldn't we at least put Ernie in the bedroom? I can't bear to look at him, sitting there with his face in his soup.

KONRAD. Good idea. We should move him now, before rigor sets in.

O'KARMA. Please, Dr. Leimgruber, we must not. It is too soon. If we disturb the body, the spirit may flee as well. Now, if you will all close your your eyes –

*(They do.)*

FATHER GERALD. Wait a minute – I hear a voice. It's Harry Houdini! He wants to know why we're bothering him.

*(MRS. McKNIGHT, EVELYN and LEIMGRUBER laugh.)*

O'KARMA. SILENCE! *(Beat)* Now, concentrate. *(They do. MADAME O'KARMA's breathing deepens as she begins to go into a trance.)* Ernest! Ernest Fenton! Madame O'Karma beckons to you. Speak to us!

*(Suddenly the room is filled with a ghostly, anguished moan, apparently coming from underneath the table. It rises in pitch and volume, until EVELYN, FATHER GERALD and KONRAD begin to cast nervous glances at each other and about the room. The spooky music rises with the tension in the room.)*

EVELYN. What is that?
O'KARMA. Silence, please! Ernest, are you there?
ERNIE's VOICE. *(Quavering mournfully.)* Yes.

*(A sting of organ music. Gasps of surprise from KONRAD and EVELYN. FATHER GERALD snorts derisively. Throughout the following, ERNIE's VOICE continues to emanate from underneath the table. The organ music continues underneath.)*

O'KARMA. I want you to look back, Ernest. Tell us what you know about your murder.
ERNIE's VOICE.
Time's passage brought about my death
With speed I could have cheated Fate;
The weapon used to stop my breath
Turned fatal when it changed its state!

*(The organ music builds to a crescendo as ERNIE's moans fade into the distance.)*

O'KARMA. Ernest! Ernest! *(Beat)* He is gone.

*(The sound of ERNIE's VOICE returns, sped-up and backwards, as though a tape machine were being rewound. They all look puzzled. FATHER GERALD looks under the table.)*

EVELYN. What on earth is that?

O'KARMA. Oh, it is nothing. It is just Ernest's spirit departing.

FATHER GERALD. Oh, is that so? Here, I'll show you Ernie's "spirit". *(He pulls out a tape recorder from underneath the table. They all gasp. Indicating O'KARMA.)* That woman is a fraud! Here's how she conjured Ernie up.

*(He pushes a button on the tape recorder and rewinds it. He presses again, and we hear the sound of ERNIE moaning. They all react.)*

KONRAD. Madame O'Karma, would you mind explaining this?

O'KARMA, Um, I er – I don't know who put that there. It was nothing to do with me.

*(Suddenly, the jack-o-lantern explodes with a loud bang. Everyone screams.)*

O'KARMA/HENRI. What on earth was that?

KONRAD/CHARLES. Please, stay where you are. I'll try the lights!

*(KONRAD/CHARLES turns on the room lights.)*

EVELYN/McKENZIE. What the hell was in that pumpkin – dynamite?

KONRAD/CHARLES. It was only a lightbulb. It must have shorted out.

EVELYN/McKENZIE. What a drag. Things were just getting interesting.

FATHER GERALD/ELWOOD. Yes, talk about spiritus interruptus!

O'KARMA/HENRI. What do we do now, Charles? Pick up where we left off?

CHARLES. Not much point, really. We were all but finished anyway.

EVELYN/McKENZIE. What a shame. I was beginning to find my character.

MRS. McKNIGHT/VALERIE. Nonsense. You were wonderful as Evelyn, right from the beginning.

EVELYN/McKENZIE. Thanks. You know, I could get used to being a politician. You can be as bitchy as you want and blame it on the economy! By the way, my real name's McKenzie. McKenzie Arnold.

*(She offers her hand. No longer shuffling, MRS. McKNIGHT/ VALERIE, crosses to McKENZIE, and shakes her hand.)*

MRS. McKNIGHT/VALERIE. Nice to meet you. I'm Valerie Addison. *(Indicating O'KARMA.)* And this is my sister Henriette.

O'KARMA/HENRI. Please call me Henri. *(She takes off the turban – the wig and glasses come off with it.)* Oh, excuse me, I have to take this off, I'm roasting! *(Extending her hand.)* A pleasure to meet you.

FATHER GERALD/ELWOOD. *(Taking off his collar.)* And I'm Elwood O'Callaghan.

HENRI. *The* Elwood O'Callaghan? The shipping magnate?

McKENZIE. That's him, alright.

VALERIE. Shipping magnate?

HENRI. Goodness, I had no idea we were in such illustrious company.

CHARLES. *(To HENRI and VALERIE.)* I apologize for not having made proper introductions when we first met, but of course the game prevented that.

VALERIE. Well it's a pleasure to meet all of you, at last.

ELWOOD. Good to meet you too, ladies. And congratulations on a game well played. You really got into the spirit of it, if you'll pardon the pun.

McKENZIE. Yeah, you two were terrific. If I didn't know better, I'd never have guessed this was your first time. I think we should have them back next year, Charles. They were a lot better than the Bartleys. *(She taps ERNIE/WILLY – still in his soup.)* Hey, Willy, say hi to Valerie and Henri. *(She stops.)* Willy, it's over. Time to get up. *(She shakes his shoulder. He doesn't budge.)* Willy? *(She shakes him again. He doesn't move. They look at each other in concern.)* Oh come on, stop fakin' it will ya?

HENRI. Maybe he fell asleep. He's been dead for an awfully long time.

ELWOOD. Maybe he drowned.

McKENZIE. Can you drown in a bowl of vichyssoise?

CHARLES. I think we should try moving him. *(As they move towards him.)* Come on Elwood, give me a hand here. Willy, are you alright?

*(Beat. They are on either side of him, about to lift him up when suddenly WILLY rears up, roaring, his face ghostly white from the soup. They all scream.)*

WILLY. Gotcha!

ELWOOD. For crying out loud, Willy!

VALERIE. *(Overlapping)* Good grief!

McKENZIE. *(Overlapping)* Willy, you jerk!

WILLY. *(Laughing)* Oh come on, what's Halloween without a good scare or two?

VALERIE. I'll admit you had me going for a moment. I was beginning to wonder if you were still with us.

HENRI. *(With her.)* – with us, yes. That would have been a real twist, wouldn't it? Playing a murder-mystery game with an actual corpse.

CHARLES. Valerie and Henriette, may I present the late Ernie Fenton – also known as Willy Yaskovitch.

WILLY. *(Taking a napkin and wiping the soup off his face.)* How ya doin'?

VALERIE. Very well, thank you. And congratulations. You made a very convincing body.

HENRI. *(With her.)* – body, yes.

WILLY. Thanks, ladies. *(Pulling off his bald pate and rubbing his head.)* Ah, it's so nice to have hair again.

ELWOOD. Don't get too attached to it, Willy. It doesn't last forever.

*(ELWOOD takes off his own beard and wig to reveal his own balding head.)*

CHARLES. Well, now that you've been safely returned to the land of the living, Willy, it's time to solve your murder. So, if you will all take out your notepads – *(Everyone crosses back to the table.)* I want you to write down who you think killed Ernie Fenton and how he or she did it.

WILLY. Alright, I admit it! It was suicide!

CHARLES. Careful, Willy. You could be right, you know.

WILLY. Oh yeah, I never thought of that.

VALERIE. Surely you must know who killed you.

WILLY. Nope. I have no idea. *(He pulls a little card from his pocket.)* My instructions simply said this: "Be sure to expire before you finish your soup."

CHARLES. Note that I did not instruct you to expire *into* your soup.

WILLY. No, but you're always telling us to improvise. I thought it was a nice touch on my part.

CHARLES. Now when you're finished, hand your answers to me. Whoever comes closest to the real solution wins.

*(During the following, people are writing their responses down.)*

HENRI. You know, Charles, I just can't believe the amount of work you put into this. Those character descriptions you sent us, for instance. All those details – right down to the medical history.

ELWOOD. Excuse me, but I failed to see the significance of Father Merriweather's hemorrhoids. Here you are.

*(He hands CHARLES his answer.)*

McKENZIE. The best part for me was getting here – all that James Bond stuff. The secret map, and that meeting in the middle of the forest –

HENRI. *(With her.)* – the forest, yes.

WILLY. Then riding over here from the mainland on that old boat, blindfolded *(Handing CHARLES his answer.)* Here you go

ELWOOD. I could have done without the blindfold, actually. That boat ride played hell with my stomach.

VALERIE. The biggest challenge for me was staying in character all that time.

HENRI. *(With her.)* – all that time, yes.

*(She and VALERIE hand CHARLES their answers.)*

CHARLES. Thanks. How about you, McKenzie? Are you ready?

McKENZIE. *(Scribbling)* Not quite.

ELWOOD. Come on, McKenzie, you're holding everything up.

McKENZIE. Alright, alright. *(She hands CHARLES her answer.)* Here you go – for what it's worth.

CHARLES. That's everybody. Now, let's find out who our winner is. I hope you've all given some thought to what you're going to ask for in the event that you've won.

*(He moves away from the others and begins to read the responses.)*

VALERIE. What we're going to ask for? I don't follow.

McKENZIE. What he means is, if you win, you get to pick your own prize.

VALERIE. Really? Like what?

WILLY. Anything we want, actually – within reason.

McKENZIE. That's why these weekends are so expensive. A big chunk of the money we put up front goes towards paying for the prize.

VALERIE. What sort of thing do you usually ask for?

WILLY. Depends on who wins, really. Remember the last time you won, McKenzie?

McKENZIE. Sure. We played Charles' version of "Murder on the Nile", and I asked for some ancient Egyptian jewelry.

ELWOOD. Yes. She pranced around for weeks afterwards pretending she was Nefertiti.

McKENZIE. And last year, the Bartleys chose that first-class trip to Monte Carlo.

WILLY. Yeah, the fools. Went and gambled away their life savings. No wonder they didn't come back this year.

CHARLES. Well, this is a first. You're not going to believe it.

WILLY. What happened, did we end up with a tie or something?

CHARLES. No, no, no. It's much better than that. This year's winner, for the first time ever, is Elwood!

McKENZIE. Elwood?

WILLY. You're kidding!

ELWOOD. *(Overlapping)* Me?

CHARLES. *(Applauding)* Congratulations, Elwood.

*(The others join in the applause.)*

ELWOOD. How do you like that? After all these years.

*(He pulls McKENZIE towards him and embraces her. She resists.)*

VALERIE. Congratulations!

HENRI. *(With her.)* – lations, yes.

CHARLES. Well done. You finally broke your losing streak.

WILLY. *(Good-naturedly)* Yeah, spoiled your perfect record.

ELWOOD. At last! I've been waiting a long time for this.

WILLY. So, any idea what you're going to ask for?

ELWOOD. Well, I've got a few thoughts.

WILLY. I should hope so. God knows you've had long enough to think about it!

HENRI. Is that how this works, Charles? Does Elwood just ask for what he wants?

CHARLES. Not just yet, Henri. First we have to complete the game. We can't have the prize until we've had the solution.

VALERIE. Yes of course, you must tell us who the murderer was.

HENRI. *(With her.)* – murderer was, yes.

WILLY. Yeah, who killed me? I've been dying to know, ha ha!

*(Groans all around.)*

CHARLES. Elwood – would you be so kind?

ELWOOD. My pleasure. It was Mrs. McKnight.

VALERIE. I killed him? You're joking. How did I do it?

ELWOOD. You poisoned his drink. Remember when you fixed us all a round?

HENRI. But everyone was drinking the same thing. How come the rest of us didn't die?

ELWOOD. Ah, but Ernie's was the only drink that was on the rocks. The poison wasn't in the drink – it was in the ice cubes.

WILLY. Of course! "The weapon used to stop my breath turned fatal when it changed its state." Very clever, Elwood.

HENRI. *(With him.)* – clever, Elwood, yes.

McKENZIE. Poisoned ice cubes. I'd never have thought of that.

CHARLES. Yes, congratulations. Nice bit of sleuthing.

ELWOOD. Thank you.

CHARLES. So would you like to tell us what you've decided on as your prize?

WILLY. Yeah, what are we going to have to cough up?

ELWOOD. *(Crossing to mantle and getting a cigar.)* Well, I'm going to need a few minutes to think about it, if that's alright with everyone.

CHARLES. Of course. Take all the time you need.

McKENZIE. In that case, I'll go and get changed. If the people at Chanel ever saw me in this get-up, they'd cancel my contract. Excuse me.

ELWOOD. Don't be too long, Darling.

McKENZIE. Of course not.

ELWOOD. You know what you're like when you get in front of a mirror.

*(She exits up the stairs. Throughout the following, the others remove what remains of their first costumes, putting them in the window box, and adding on pieces of their "real" clothes.)*

WILLY. Did you leave any food for me? I'm starving.

CHARLES. We certainly did. It's keeping warm in the oven.

HENRI. I'll go and get it for you.

WILLY. Thanks, Henriette.

*(She crosses to the panelled wall UR.)*

VALERIE. Where are you going? The kitchen's that way.

HENRI. I know, but I've been dying to try this secret panel. *(She pulls a handle [or pushes a button] and suddenly the panelling swings open like a door. She looks inside, hesitates.)* Which way do I go?

CHARLES. Just bear right. It will take you right into the pantry.

HENRI. Ooh, how marvellous!

*(She exits.)*

WILLY. What is that, a servants' passage or something?

CHARLES. I imagine. It goes all over the house. It'll even take you upstairs.

WILLY. Man, this place is great. It's like something right out of Agatha Christie!

ELWOOD. That's no surprise. Everything Charles does is like something out of Agatha Christie. Haven't you ever read any of his novels?

*(CHARLES picks up the gun/lighter and re-lights his cigar.)*

CHARLES. Are you implying that my books are derivative, Elwood?

ELWOOD. I wouldn't go that far. Let's just say it's not hard to see where your inspiration comes from. *(Indicating the picture of Agatha hanging above the fireplace.)* I mean, you take the poor woman with you wherever you go, for heaven's sake!

VALERIE. Well, it doesn't matter to me where you got the idea from, I thought the game was brilliant.

CHARLES. Thank you, Valerie.

VALERIE. But of course, I am a little biased. Henri and I have been big fans of yours for years. We've read everything you've written. I must confess, when she told me we had been invited to spend the weekend playing a murder mystery game hosted by Charles Prince himself, I couldn't believe it. I thought she must be pulling my leg.

CHARLES. Well, I hope meeting me in the flesh hasn't been too much of a disappointment for you.

VALERIE. On the contrary. It's been delightful. But it must be a bit of a busman's holiday for you. I mean, creating a game like this must be almost as much work as writing one of your mystery novels. One would think you'd get tired of all that death and destruction.

ELWOOD. *(Crossing to the mantelpiec.)* No, no. Murder and mayhem, that's what Charles lives for. That's why he keeps coming up with these games every Halloween.

VALERIE. Every Halloween? How long have you been doing this?

CHARLES. As a matter of fact, this is our tenth anniversary.

VALERIE. Ten years? That's a long time. What got you started?

CHARLES. Well, ever since I first came here I was captivated by the idea of Halloween. You see it just isn't celebrated in England the way it is in North America. I couldn't believe what I'd been missing all my life. So after my first Halloween here, I decided I would make up for lost time. The very next year I wrote the first game, turned my home into a haunted house for the evening, *(He gestures to the WILLY and ELWOOD.)* and invited a few friends to dress up and participate.

WILLY. It was a blast.

CHARLES. Yes, it was a rousing success, if I do say so myself. In fact, we all had so much fun, we decided to make it an annual event.

*(McKENZIE enters down the stairs, now dressed in a glamorous and somewhat revealing dress.)*

McKENZIE. Ta-daa! How's that for a quick change?

CHARLES. Goodness.

WILLY. That's quite the dress, McKenzie.

McKENZIE. *(Preening)* Do you like it?

CHARLES. It's stunning.

McKENZIE. Isn't it? I got it from that Vogue shoot I was on last week in Paris.

ELWOOD. Er, Darling, I thought I asked you not to bring that dress with you this weekend.

McKENZIE. But Elwood, I haven't had a chance to wear it yet.

ELWOOD. Yes, but it's not exactly appropriate for the occasion, now is it? Don't you have anything a little less – showy?

McKENZIE. Not really.

ELWOOD. What about the black outfit?

McKENZIE. Oh, Elwood, you always want me to wear that.

ELWOOD. Only because you look so lovely in it, Darling. Now be a good girl and go and put it on, alright?

McKENZIE. *(Protesting)* Elwood –

ELWOOD. Just do it, will you, McKenzie?

McKENZIE. *(After a beat.)* Alright.

*(She hoists up her dress and trudges up the stairs. There is an awkward pause.)*

VALERIE. What a lovely-looking girl. Have you been married long?

ELWOOD. Oh, we're not married.

VALERIE. I'm sorry. I just assumed –

ELWOOD. That's alright.

*(Suddenly there is a scream from behind the secret panel.)*

WILLY. What was that?

*(CHARLES and VALERIE cross to the secret panel.)*

VALERIE. It sounded like Henri. *(CHARLES opens the panel. HENRI enters, carrying a plate covered by a silver plate-warmer. She is terrified. VALERIE takes the plate from her.)* Are you alright?

HENRI. There's something in there.

VALERIE. What are you talking about?

HENRI. I was coming back from the kitchen and I felt something behind me.

CHARLES. How odd. Let's have a look.

*(CHARLES goes into the passage to investigate.)*

ELWOOD. What are you saying? Do you mean there's someone in there?

HENRI. Not someone – some*thing.*

VALERIE. What kind of something?

HENRI. I don't know.

VALERIE. Henri, you're imagining things.

HENRI. It was cold, like something out of the grave.

WILLY. Maybe it was Casper the friendly ghost, trying to cop a quick feel!

HENRI. It's not a joke, Willy.

*(CHARLES re-enters.)*

CHARLES. There's nothing in there, my dear. Just a lot of old cobwebs.

ELWOOD. There you go, Henri. That's probably all it was.

HENRI. No, I swear, there was something in there.

VALERIE. It was nothing Henriette. Now pull yourself together.

HENRI. But I fealt it, Valerie –

VALERIE. That's enough! *(HENRI lowers her head.)* Please excuse Henri. She's always been a little on the sensitive side. She used to be horribly afraid of the dark when she was a child. I'd sometimes have to sit up and read to her for hours before she'd go to sleep.

HENRI. *(Embarrassed)* Valerie, please.

VALERIE. Anyway, here's your dinner, Willy. Bon appetit.

WILLY. *(Lifting up the plate-warmer.)* Thanks. Mmm, this looks great.

VALERIE. Oh it's delicious.

ELWOOD. Yes, you outdid yourself this year, Charles. Quite a feast.

VALERIE. You mean, you did the cooking as well?

WILLY. Yeah, Charles does everything.

ELWOOD. A man of many talents, is our Charles. *(Calling)* McKenzie, where are you?

McKENZIE. *(Off)* Coming!

VALERIE. *(To CHARLES.)* Well I have to say, despite Henri's ghosts in the passageway, I've had a marvellous day. Thank you so much for inviting us.

CHARLES. Not at all – only too happy to have you. When the Bartleys told me what mystery buffs you two were, I knew this sort of thing would be just your cup of tea.

VALERIE. The Bartleys?

HENRI. Yes, you know the Bartleys. Margaret and I are on the board together at the Emmerson Art Gallery. I introduced you to them at the Humphrey exhibition last year. Don't you remember?

VALERIE. No, I don't.

CHARLES. Well they remembered you. When they called to tell me they couldn't make it, I asked if they knew of anyone else who might be interested, and they immediately suggested you.

HENRI. Well, I'm very glad they did. *(With a look to the secret panel.)* I think.

VALERIE. Yes, I couldn't imagine a more appropriate way to spend Halloween.

CHARLES. And it's not over yet. We still have to determine what Elwood has won.

WILLY. Yeah, we've had the tricks, now it's time for the treats!

ELWOOD. What the hell is taking her so long? *(Calling)* McKenzie, what are you doing up there?

McKENZIE. *(Off)* Be right there.

*(CHARLES crosses to the drinks table and picks up a bottle of brandy from a lower shelf.)*

CHARLES. Some brandy, Henri?
HENRI. Yes, please.
CHARLES. *(Proffering the bottle.)* Valerie?
VALERIE. Yes, thank you.

*(McKENZIE comes running down the stairs in a much more modest outfit.)*

ELWOOD. Ah, there you are.
McKENZIE. Sorry to keep you.
CHARLES. Brandy, McKenzie?
McKENZIE. Thanks.

*(CHARLES hands McKENZIE and HENRI each a drink. He then puts the bottle back on the lower shelf and pours a drink from the decanter. He hands this drink to VALERIE.)*

CHARLES. Now, in keeping with our tradition, I'd like to propose a toast. If you would all stand and raise your glasses – *(All but WILLY stand up. CHARLES turns and faces the portrait above the fireplace.)* To the woman who inspired our love of mysteries in the first place – that dowager of dramatic mystery, that matriarch of murder, that heroine of the whodunnit – Agatha Christie!

*(They all turn to the portrait and raise their glasses.)*

ALL. To Agatha!

*(Suddenly the passageway door opens slowly with a loud creak. They all react. HENRI gasps and backs away.)*

HENRI. I told you there was something in there!

CHARLES. *(Crossing to the panel and closing the door.)* Come now, let's not read too much into this. The latch probably just gave way.

HENRI. I'm not so sure.

VALERIE. Oh come on, Henriette. Your little scare in the passageway has got your imagination working overtime.

McKENZIE. What scare in the passageway?

WILLY. Henri thought she saw a ghost.

HENRI. I didn't say it was a ghost.

VALERIE. Oh, Henri. You've been reading too much Stephen King.

HENRI. It's this place. There's something awfully spooky about it. It gives me the willies.

*(Everyone looks at WILLY.)*

WILLY. So to speak.

ELWOOD. *(In an attempt to lighten the mood.)* Well it certainly scores full points for atmosphere.

VALERIE. Indeed. I've been meaning to ask you, Charles – how did you find it?

CHARLES. Oh, through one of those real estate brochures, you know.

McKENZIE. What was it listed under? Haunted Houses for rent?

CHARLES. Holiday homes, actually. It was quite a catchy advertisement – said something like, "Haddington House – secluded summer home perched on a cliff on private island in the Cassandra Lakes."

HENRI. Cassandra Lakes?

*(VALERIE puts a warning hand on HENRI's shoulder.)*

ELWOOD. Cassandra Lakes! So that's where we are.

CHARLES. But it was the line at the end that really caught my eye. In bold print it read: "Not for the faint-hearted."

WILLY. *(Imitating the spooky organ music.)* Ooo-ooo-ooo-ooo-ooo!

CHARLES. It sounded ideal, so I rented it.

ELWOOD. It's certainly perfect for our purposes.

WILLY. *(Indicating window R.)* And you got to love the view.

CHARLES. Yes. I would have opened the shutters on all the windows, but they warned me that this place gets awfully draughty this time of year. It's really only intended for summer use.

WILLY. I'm glad you opened this one, anyway. That was some sunset.

McKENZIE. What do you suppose they meant by "not for the faint-hearted?"

ELWOOD. They probably meant that climb up from the dock. It just about did me in.

CHARLES. I think it was just an advertising ploy, actually. They like to play up the mystery angle around here. It helps the tourist trade.

McKENZIE. The mystery angle?

CHARLES. Yes, you know. The Phantom Five. They were rumoured to have disappeared somewhere in this area.

McKENZIE. Who were the Phantom Five?

*(HENRI and VALERIE exchange another look.)*

WILLY. Oh come on, Mack. Don't you read anything except fashion magazines? You must have heard of them. They were the biggest disappearing act since Amelia Earhardt.

CHARLES. It was a famous case about twenty-odd years ago. It's never been solved. Five very wealthy, influential people with no apparent connection to one another suddenly vanished at the same time.

WILLY. People have been trying to figure out what happened to them for years. Some people think they were killed in a boating accident, some say they were taken out by the mob; some people even think they went off and joined a religious cult.

HENRI. Nonsense!

VALERIE. *(Cautioning her.)* Henri –

McKENZIE. So what does all this have to do with the Cassandra Lakes?

ELWOOD. The only connection is that on the day of their disappearance, all five of them were seen arriving at a private airstrip in the Cassandra Lakes area. They were never seen again.

McKENZIE. Really. No wonder you're seeing ghosts, Henri.

CHARLES. Anyway, that's all ancient history; and we still have some unfinished business to attend to – Elwood's prize.

WILLY. Yeah, I almost forgot. What's it going to be, Elwood?

ELWOOD. *(Lightly)* Well, as you so nicely pointed out, Willy, I've had a long time to think about this; and I decided years ago that if I ever did win one of these games, I'd want my prize to be something – a little out of the ordinary. Something that would require a bit of creativity on my part. And I think I've finally hit on the perfect idea: What I would like ... is a favour from each of you.

WILLY. A favour?

ELWOOD. Yes.

McKENZIE. What does that mean, exactly?

WILLY. You mean you get to borrow my power tools? Or drive Charles' Jag convertible for the weekend?

ELWOOD. If that's the sort of thing I choose to ask for, yes.

McKENZIE. That's it? Doesn't sound like much of a prize to me.

*(ELWOOD crosses to pour himself another drink.)*

HENRI. I'm not sure I understand. What is it you're asking of us, exactly?

ELWOOD. It's very simple. I'm saying that I get to ask one favour of each of you, and you're obligated to do it. Whatever it is.

CHARLES. One favour each.

ELWOOD. Of my choice. That's right.

WILLY. Wait a second. Anything? You can ask for anything you want?

ELWOOD. Yes.

WILLY. And we've got to give it to you?

ELWOOD. Correct. You've grasped the concept admirably.

WILLY. No restrictions, no exceptions?

ELWOOD. None.

WILLY. Oh my God.

*(ELWOOD crosses to the fireplace.)*

ELWOOD. *(Chuckling)* Yes, this is going to be fun.

*(He picks up a cigar from the humidor on the mantle, crosses to the table and lights his cigar with the gun/lighter.)*

WILLY. I don't like it. I think it's a bad idea.

HENRI. Why? It seems harmless enough to me.

WILLY. Harmless? What are you talking about? It's worth a fortune.

HENRI. How so?

WILLY. He's written himself a blank cheque! Suppose he asks me to hand over everything I own?

ELWOOD. Oh, come on. I won 147 companies around the world. I don't need anything of yours.

WILLY. Who said anything about need?

CHARLES. Willy, it's only a game, remember. Anyway, Elwood is aware of our budget. He knows we can't give him anything too extravagant.

WILLY. It's not the money I'm worried about. What if he asks me to rob a bank? Am I expected to go out and do it?

ELWOOD. Don't you think you're over-reacting just a bit, Willy?

HENRI. I think it's very clever. I mean, winning a trip to Monte Carlo is all very nice, but this is much more imaginative.

ELWOOD. Exactly! *(With an arm around McKENZIE.)* Of course, for some of you, deciding what to ask for won't take too much imagination at all.

*(McKENZIE smiles half-heartedly.)*

CHARLES. I'm sure we can count on Elwood to keep his requests within reason.

WILLY. Can we?

VALERIE. Look, if you're so concerned about it, why don't we just ask Elwood what he wants of us?

CHARLES. Good idea.

WILLY. Yes, let's get this over with. *(Turning to ELWOOD.)* OK, Elwood? What's it going to be?

ELWOOD. I beg your pardon?

WILLY. Your favour. Don't keep us in suspense. Tell us what you want.

ELWOOD. Well I don't know yet. I wasn't exactly prepared to win the game, you know. I need some time to think.

WILLY. How much time, exactly?

ELWOOD. Be reasonable. Part of the fun of a prize like this is figuring out what you're going to do with it.

McKENZIE. Oh, God.

WILLY. I'm telling you right now, Elwood. You take this too far, and I'm not going along with it.

ELWOOD. Don't be such a poor sport. You don't hear any of the others complaining, do you?

WILLY. It's got nothing to do with being a poor sport. I just don't think it's fair to expect us to sit here indefinitely, wondering when the axe is going to fall. *(Turning to CHARLES.)* I want to know what he wants, and I want to know now!

McKENZIE. Willy, cool your jets, will you? You're just going to make things worse.

ELWOOD. Alright people, I tell you what I'll do. In the interests of good sportsmanship, I'm going to go upstairs right now and make my decisions. You'll all have your requests before the night is out. Will that satisfy you? *(WILLY says nothing. ELWOOD crosses to the staircase.)* Very well then.

*(He exits.)*

WILLY. And what are we supposed to do in the meantime – sit here and play tiddlywinks?

CHARLES. Calm down, Willy. What's the matter with you?

WILLY. Look, I just know what Elwood's like, alright? I worked with the man, I've seen how he treats people. You think he got to own 147 companies by being a nice guy?

VALERIE. Yes, but that's business. You have to be tough in business if you want to survive.

McKENZIE. I don't know, Willy, maybe you are jumping to conclusions a bit. Why don't we wait and see what he asks for?

WILLY. Oh come on, Mack. Back me up here. You know what he's like as well as I do.

HENRI. You don't really think Elwood would ask us to do anything – unsavoury, do you?

WILLY. That's exactly what I think.

VALERIE. But why would he? He doesn't even know Henri and me. What could he possibly want from us that would be so unpleasant?

HENRI. *(With her.)* – so unpleasant, yes?

WILLY. Frankly, I'm not sticking around to find out.

VALERIE. What do you mean?

WILLY. I mean I'm getting out of here.

McKENZIE. You're not serious.

WILLY. You better believe I'm serious. Where's my chair?

McKENZIE. Come on Willy. Think it over, will you?

WILLY. I've thought it over. Where the hell is my chair?

McKENZIE. Running away is no answer. You should know that better than anybody.

WILLY. Will somebody get me my damn chair?

McKENZIE. *(Sighs)* Yes, alright. It's in your room.

*(McKENZIE exits UR.)*

CHARLES. Don't you think you're being a little premature? Why don't you give him the benefit of the doubt? I'm sure all he wants is a bit of fun.

WILLY. That's what I'm worried about, Charles. His definition of fun and yours are two very different things. I'm telling you, he's a dangerous man.

HENRI. You're starting to frighten me, Willy.

WILLY. Well it's nice to know I'm getting through to somebody.

CHARLES. Alright, that's enough! There's no point in alarming people unnecessarily.

WILLY. Fine, but don't say I didn't warn you. Now, how the hell do I get out of here?

HENRI. Willy, please, you can't leave!

CHARLES. That's right. You *can't* leave, I'm afraid. The boat's back on the mainland, and it's not scheduled to pick us up until tomorrow.

WILLY. Can't you call somebody? Tell them one of your guests is going home early?

CHARLES. No, I'm sorry. There's no phone here.

WILLY. Well, hasn't someone brought a cell phone with them, at least?

CHARLES. Even if they did, it wouldn't work. There's no service in this area.

WILLY. There's got to be some way off this rock!

CHARLES. Not unless you fancy a two-and-a-half-mile swim.

*(McKENZIE enters UR with wheelchair.)*

WILLY. Shit. You mean I'm stuck here?

CHARLES. That's right, so you might as well make the most of it.

McKENZIE. Here you go, Willy.

*(She helps him into the wheelchair.)*

WILLY. Well, maybe you can make me stay, but you can't make me go along with this.

CHARLES. Can't you at least wait until you've heard Elwood's request?

VALERIE. Yes. I mean. if it's that unreasonable, you can just refuse to do it.

HENRI. *(With him.)* – do it, yes.

WILLY. Not according to Elwood. He can ask for whatever he wants – and we have to give it to him.

CHARLES. Within reason, of course. Elwood wouldn't take advantage of us. He's an old friend after all.

WILLY. He's no friend of mine.

CHARLES. Well, I still think we should wait and see what he asks for. If anyone has any strong objections, I'm sure Elwood will be happy to change his request.

ELWOOD. Don't bet on it.

*(Everyone turns to see ELWOOD standing in the entrance to the secret passage.)*

McKENZIE. Elwood!

ELWOOD. I'm surprised at you, Charles. To think you'd even suggest such a thing. I thought you had more integrity than that.

WILLY. Elwood –

ELWOOD. Shut up, Yaskovitch. I've heard enough out of you. *(To the others.)* I've waited ten years for this, and I'm not going to be cheated out of it now. If you don't like what I ask for, that's just too bad. You're going to have to pay up anyhow.

WILLY. What if we refuse?

ELWOOD. Oh you'll pay, Willy – *(He pulls out a gun and levels it at WILLY.)* one way or another.

CHARLES. Elwood, what on earth are you doing?

ELWOOD. Just making my point. I won the game – now I'm collecting what I'm owed – and I *will* collect. *(Brandishing the gun at them.)* Understood? *(Silence)* Good. In that case, I think I'll call it a night. *(ELWOOD turns and heads towards the stairs. He stops, turns and smiles.)* Sweet dreams.

*(He exits. They all watch him go. Suddenly CHARLES bursts into applause, laughing as he does so.)*

CHARLES. What a performance!

VALERIE. Performance? What do you mean? He certainly looked as though he meant business.

HENRI. *(With her.)* – business, yes.

CHARLES. Oh come now. What did you think he was going to do? Commit mass murder with a cigarette lighter?

VALERIE. Cigarette lighter?

CHARLES. Yes, of course! I must admit, he was rather good. He even had me going for a moment.

VALERIE. You don't mean ... ? Oh, that old prankster!

HENRI. *(With her.)* – prankster!

McKENZIE. What a slimy stunt to pull – threatening us with a lighter!

*(They laugh.)*

WILLY. That was no lighter.

*(Everyone turns to WILLY.)*

CHARLES. What do you mean?
WILLY. Look.

*(WILLY holds up the gun/lighter and pulls the trigger. A small flame shoots out the end. BLACKOUT.)*

### *Scene Two*

*(Setting: The same as above. Night – a few hours later. The table and some of the chairs have been struck. The curtains have been drawn across the window DR. A storm is raging outside. The only source of light is from the fireplace. There is a banging sound from the window area. HENRI, dressed in her nightclothes, appears at the top of the stairs.)*

HENRI. Hello? Is anyone there? *(She comes down the stairs a bit, peering through the gloom, stops. There is a second bang from the window.)* Valerie, is that you? *(She reaches the bottom of the stairs. There is another loud bang from the direction of the window R. HENRI freezes in her tracks.)* Who's there?

*(HENRI crosses to the fireplace and picks up a poker. She brandishes it as she crosses toward the window DR, poker at the ready. She raises the poker, reaches slowly toward the curtains when suddenly they are flung open. There is a flash of lightning as VALERIE is revealed standing on the window seat. They both scream. HENRI steps back.)*

VALERIE. *(Startled)* Oh, Henriette! You scared me to death.
HENRI. *(Startled)* I scared you? What are you doing up there?

*(VALERIE, also in her nightclothes, steps down off the window seat and crosses to HENRI.)*

VALERIE. I was just trying to close the window. Goodness, look at me, I'm soaked. *(VALERIE crosses to the drinks table, turns on a lamp and gets a small towel to dry herself off.)* What are you doing with that poker?
HENRI. *(Crossing to replace it.)* I was frightened. It sounded like someone was trying to break in.
VALERIE. Well I'm glad you're up. I was just about to wake you anyway.
HENRI. Really? Why?

*(She turns on another light. There is a crack of thunder.)*

VALERIE. You'd better sit down, Henriette. I have something here I'd like to read to you.
HENRI. But Valerie, I've –
VALERIE. Sit down. I think you should hear this. *(She pulls a note from her pocket, opens it up and reads, pacing as she does so.)* "To The Addison Sisters, Valerie and Henriette: It has recently come to my attention that your company, Addison Utilities, has knowingly been leaking toxic waste into the surrounding water supply. My request to you is that on Monday morning, you make public your outrageous disregard for the environment. Yours Truly, Elwood O'Callaghan." Did you know anything about this?
HENRI. *(Holding up a note of her own.)* Yes, I've already read it.

VALERIE. I'm not talking about the letter. I'm talking about Addison Utilities polluting the local water supply.

HENRI. Well yes, I knew about it, but –

VALERIE. Then why didn't you tell me?

HENRI. I only found out about it a couple of months ago.

VALERIE. A couple of months? You mean, you've known for months that our company was poisoning the area and it didn't occur to you to mention it?

HENRI. Well, no. I thought – I thought it best to keep it quiet. The fewer people who knew about it the better.

VALERIE. *(Apoplectic)* I'm the President and CEO of Addison Utilities. *Nothing* goes on in my company without my knowing about it. Do you understand?

HENRI. *(Quietly)* It's my company too, Valerie.

VALERIE. There wouldn't be a company if it weren't for me, Henriette. And there probably won't be one for much longer, thanks to your stupidity. Do you have any idea what will happen when this gets out? It'll be the end of Addison Utilities! It'll cost us millions! I can't believe it. After all I've done to promote this company as a responsible corporate citizen. I'm on the board of every environmental group in the area, for God's sake!

HENRI. Keep your voice down –

VALERIE. Don't tell me to keep my voice down!

HENRI. We don't want to wake everyone up.

VALERIE. *(Lowering her voice.)* What in God's name did you think you were doing?

HENRI. I was trying to take care of it on my own. I was planning to tell you all about it as soon as the clean-up was complete. I wanted to show you I could handle a crisis like this.

VALERIE. And now you know that you can't. I hope you're satisfied.

HENRI. But the clean-up was already in progress. Another few weeks and it would have been over and done with. I had it under control.

VALERIE. Did you really? Then perhaps you could explain why Elwood seems to know all about it?

HENRI. I have no idea. I was very careful about the security arrangements.

VALERIE. Not careful enough, apparently. Thanks to your incompetence, we can kiss our company goodbye!

HENRI. *(Trying not to cry.)* It's not my fault. It's Elwood who's put us in this position.

VALERIE. Don't start blubbering, for Heaven's sake. We have to decide what we're going to do.

*(There is a clap of thunder. The lights flicker.)*

HENRI. Why would he want to do something like this? We haven't done him any harm. We've only just met him!

VALERIE. You're so naïve. He obviously wants to take over our company. Once this news becomes public, we won't be able to give our stock away. Elwood will be able to step in and buy it at a fraction of its value.

HENRI. What does he want with Addison Utilities? He already has a hundred and forty-something companies of his own!

VALERIE. Well now we know how he got those, don't we?

HENRI. It looks like Willy knew what he was talking about. We should have listened to him.

VALERIE. We should have stayed at home, that's what we should have done. I don't know why I let you talk me into this stupid weekend.

HENRI. Oh, Valerie, that's not fair. I didn't talk you into anything. When you heard about it, you wanted to come as much as I did.

VALERIE. *(Holding up note.)* And as if finding ourselves at Cassandra Lakes wasn't bad enough, now we have this to contend with.

HENRI. You can't blame me for that. I had no way of knowing where Charles was going to bring us. This was as much a surprise to me as it was to you.

VALERIE. If only *I* had won that stupid game.

HENRI. Look, why don't we talk to Elwood, see if we can reason with him? Perhaps we can reach some sort of compromise.

VALERIE. He's not going to compromise.

HENRI. But surely it must be against the rules to demand

something like this. Didn't Charles say that the prize can't exceed the budget? Addison Utilities is worth millions!

VALERIE. It doesn't look as though Elwood cares very much about the rules. In any case, he hasn't asked us to give him Addison Utilities. All he's asked us to do is make a statement. And you heard what he said would happen if we didn't go along with his request.

HENRI. You don't really think he meant it, do you?

VALERIE. He was pointing a gun at us, Henriette, of course he meant it!

HENRI. Do you honestly believe he could get rid of us that easily?

VALERIE. It wouldn't be that hard to make five people disappear. It's happened before, hasn't it? Don't forget where we are.

HENRI. Oh my God. What are we going to do?

VALERIE. We have no choice. We're going to have to do what Elwood wants. *(There is a crash. HENRI and VALERIE are startled.)* Who's there?

HENRI. *(At the same time.)* What was that?

*(McKENZIE appears from the archway, in a bathrobe, her hair wrapped up in a towel.)*

McKENZIE. Sorry ladies, it's only me. I tripped over some fishing tackle.

VALERIE. What brings you down here, McKenzie?

McKENZIE. Oh, I was just having a bath.

HENRI. In the middle of the night?

McKENZIE. That room of mine is freezing, I couldn't get warm. Gee, it's awful gloomy in here. Do you mind if I turn on another light? *(She goes over to one of the side tables, turns on a lamp.)* Not interrupting anything, am I?

VALERIE. Not at all.

HENRI. *(With her.)* – at all, no.

*(A loud clap of thunder. McKENZIE starts.)*

McKENZIE. God, I need a drink. I can't stand storms. *(Looking down.)* What's this? *(Picks up a letter from the drinks table.)* Hey, it's addressed to me! Well, that's one way of making sure I'd find it – leaving it next to the scotch bottle.

*(She tears the letter open and reads it.)*

HENRI. It's from Elwood, isn't it?

McKENZIE. How did you know?

HENRI. *(Holding up the letter.)* We got one too.

VALERIE. Well, you shouldn't have much to worry about. I can't see Elwood asking anything too onerous of you.

McKENZIE. Oh shit.

VALERIE. What is it?

McKENZIE. That son of a bitch!

VALERIE. What does it say?

HENRI. *(With her.)* – say, McKenzie?

McKENZIE. *(Snaps)* It's none of your business. *(She puts the letter into her pocket. Another crack of thunder. McKENZIE reacts.)* Sorry, ladies. I didn't mean to bark at you.

HENRI. It's alright. We know how you feel.

McKENZIE. Do you? *(She turns and pours herself a large drink. A loud clap of thunder. Startled, McKENZIE spills the liquor.)* Dammit!

HENRI. Goodness, that storm is getting closer.

McKENZIE. Sounds as if it's right on top of us. God, I wish I could get the hell out of here.

VALERIE. My feelings exactly. This weekend is not turning out at all the way I expected.

McKENZIE. Me neither.

HENRI. Have you ever had anything like this happen at any of your other games?

McKENZIE. No, never! But then no one's ever come up with a prize like this before. *(Another crack of thunder. McKENZIE starts.)* Well, if this is going to go on all night, I might as well find myself something decent to read. Let's see what we have here. *(She crosses to the bookshelves and scans the titles.)* "Ulyooo", "A Tale of Two Cities", "Anna Karen-neena"? Oh, please.

HENRI. What's wrong? Not your cup of tea?

McKENZIE. I was hoping for something with more pictures, actually. Anybody got a Vanity Fair? *(HENRI and VALERIE look at her blankly.)* No, I guess not. *(She finds a book on the shelf.)* Oh, this'll do nicely. "And Then There Were None", by Agatha Christie. *(As she pulls out the book from a lower shelf, a hidden compartment on an upper shelf opens.)* Hey, check this out!

*(She puts the book back and the compartment closes. She pulls the book out again and it opens.)*

HENRI. Good heavens!

VALERIE. How extraordinary.

McKENZIE. Well, well, well, what do we have here? *(She reaches in to the compartment and pulls out a leather-bound book about the size of a photo album. She crosses down to VALERIE and HENRI as she blows the dust off it. She flips through the book.)* Looks like some sort of journal.

*(There is a monstrous clap of thunder. The lights flicker and go out.)*

HENRI. What's happened to the lights?

McKENZIE. The storm must have knocked the power out.

HENRI. Oh no!

McKENZIE. Terrific. That's all we need.

VALERIE. Whatever next?

McKENZIE. I'll see if I can find a flashlight. *(She carefully crosses UR to the bookcase and starts rummaging around.)* There's gotta be one around here somewhere. Aha! Here we go. *(She pulls out a flashlight, turns it on, crosses slightly DS. It shines directly on WILLY, who is sitting inches away from her, dressed in sweats and slumped in his wheelchair with his tongue hanging out.)* Willy!

*(WILLY suddenly looks up at her.)*

WILLY. Boo!

*(McKENZIE, VALERIE and HENRI all scream. Another clap of thunder.)*

McKENZIE. You jerk!

WILLY. *(In a Boris Karloff voice.)* "It was a dark and stormy night ..."

VALERIE. I wish you'd stop doing things like that.

HENRI. *(With her.)* – like that, yes. We're all frightened enough as it is without your help.

McKENZIE. What are you doing up, anyway?

WILLY. Are you kidding? You'd have to be dead to sleep through this.

McKENZIE. Well as long as you're here, you might as well make yourself useful. Hold this for me, will you?

*(McKENZIE hands WILLY the flashlight and starts lighting a number of candles with the gun/lighter, placing them around the room.)*

WILLY. *(Inspecting the book.)* What is this?

HENRI. It's a journal of some kind. McKenzie found it in a secret compartment in the bookcase!

WILLY. Secret compartment, eh? Boy, this place has everything, doesn't it? *(A loud crash of thunder. HENRI gasps.)* Hey, settle down, Henri.

HENRI. I'm sorry. It's this place. It's getting to me. First there was the exploding pumpkin, then that thing in the passageway, and now the power's gone out. I feel as though I'm in the middle of some horror story.

WILLY. Oh this is nothing. I could tell you a real horror story – the year I played for the Lions.

McKENZIE. I wouldn't exactly call that a horror story.

WILLY. You obviously didn't see us play!

McKENZIE. Did you know that Willy used to be a big football star?

HENRI. Really?

WILLY. Oh, that's old news. I retired years ago.

McKENZIE. Not before he collected two MVP awards and had a couple of schools named after him.

HENRI. My goodness. It sounds like you had quite a career. You must miss it.

WILLY. Miss what? Getting pounded into the ground by a bunch of Neanderthals every Sunday afternoon?

McKENZIE. Don't let him kid you, Henri. He loved playing the game.

WILLY. Well, I suppose it beat sitting at home watching it on TV.

McKENZIE. Now you're just another armchair quarterback.

WILLY. Wheelchair quarterback, you mean.

*(Beat)*

VALERIE. Is that how you injured yourself? Playing football?

WILLY. *(Indicating wheelchair.)* You mean this? Oh hell, no. This just happened six months ago. Car accident.

VALERIE. Oh, I'm sorry.

WILLY. Hey, look at the bright side – now I get all the best parking spaces.

HENRI. Oh, Willy.

McKENZIE. *(Crossing to WILLY with a candle.)* Now give me that journal, and let's have a look at what we've found. *(He hands her the book. She flips to the front page and starts to read.)* There's an introduction here. Hey, listen to this – "The following is a complete account of the meetings of 'The Mousetrap Society', as recorded by Colin Jeffries." There's a list of members – "Ronald Roberts, Donald Ewes, Mara English, Colin Jeffries and Hank Addison."

*(HENRI gasps.)*

VALERIE. Oh my God.

*(VALERIE sits down hard on the couch.)*

HENRI. *(Crossing to her.)* Oh, Valerie!

McKENZIE. What's the matter? You look like you've seen a ghost.

HENRI. Hank Addison. He was our father.

*(Crack of thunder.)*

McKENZIE. No kidding! Your dad was a member of this Mousetrap Society?

HENRI. That's what it looks like.

McKENZIE. That's amazing!

WILLY. McKenzie – those names you just read out – they're not just the members of this Mousetrap Society; they're also the Phantom Five!

*(There is a crack of thunder.)*

McKENZIE. You're joking. *(To HENRI and VALERIE.)* Your old man was one of the Phantom Five? How come you never said anything when we were talking about it before?

HENRI. Well, it's not the sort of thing we like to advertise. We've had enough attention from the media over the years.

WILLY. Yeah, I guess you must have.

McKENZIE. Let me get this straight. You didn't know your father was a part of this "Mousetrap Society"?

HENRI. No. This is the first time we've heard of it, isn't it, Valerie?

VALERIE. *(Crossing to McKENZIE.)* What does the book say, McKenzie?

McKENZIE. It seems to be a record of yearly meetings. See the dates? It looks like they got together every Halloween and played mystery games. Now doesn't that sound familiar? *(Flipping through the journal.)* Ooh, look. At the beginning of each game there's a picture of the place where they went to play. Here's one in Tahiti. Hmm. These guys sure got around.

VALERIE. May I see that for a moment, please? *(VALERIE takes the book.)* Good God. The last game in the book was dated October 31st 1973.

WILLY. Twenty five years ago, to the day.

HENRI. *(Crossing to VALERIE.)* That's the day Daddy disappeared! Does it say anything about where it took place?

VALERIE. Well there's a picture here  oh my God.

HENRI. What is it?

VALERIE. The last game took place here – at Haddington House!

*(There is a monstrous clap of thunder.)*

HENRI. What? Let me see. *(Taking the book from VALERIE.)* This is incredible. You mean we're staying in the very place where Daddy disappeared? No wonder I've been having such strange feelings about this house. Valerie, do you realize what this means? After all these years, we may finally be able to find out what happened to Daddy! Valerie, are you alright?

VALERIE. Yes, yes, I'm fine. I just – I just can't believe it.

*(HENRI surreptitiously takes the picture from the journal.)*

WILLY. I don't get it. Why has Charles been keeping this to himself for so long?

HENRI. *(Putting the picture in her pocket.)* You think Charles knew about the journal?

WILLY. Well of course. Look at the similarities between us and this Mousetrap Society – getting together every Halloween, playing murder mystery games, even the Agatha Christie connection ... Charles obviously got the idea from this journal, so he must have had it for years.

HENRI. *(With him.)* – years, yes.

McKENZIE. Kind of makes me wonder what other ideas Charles got from that journal.

VALERIE. What do you mean?

McKENZIE. This whole thing is beginning to smell very fishy to me. I mean, why did Charles bring us here, of all places? It can't just be an accident that you two find yourselves in the very place where your father disappeared.

VALERIE. What do you suppose he's planning to do with us? *(Suddenly, we hear a loud knocking. They all look at each other.)* What on earth is that?

*(There is another knock.)*

HENRI. Oh God.
WILLY. Listen! It's coming from over there.

*(He indicates the window seat. McKENZIE crosses anxiously to the window. There is another knock, coming from beneath the window seat.)*

McKENZIE. There's someone in here!

*(McKENZIE, with no small measure of trepidation, lifts the lid on the window seat. CHARLES, dazed, with blood dripping down his face, is discovered underneath. McKENZIE helps him as he struggles to his feet.)*

WILLY. Charles!
VALERIE. *(Overlapping)* My goodness. Are you alright?

*(CHARLES tries to stand, stumbles. McKENZIE helps him out of the window seat.)*

McKENZIE. Here, you'd better sit down.

*(She helps him to a chair.)*

HENRI. What happened, Charles?
CHARLES. I don't really know. I was just getting into bed when I heard some strange sounds down here. I came down to investigate and I was just about to turn on the lights when someone hit me over the head.

McKENZIE. Did you see who it was?
CHARLES. No. It was dark, and whoever it was managed to knock me out before I could get a look at them. It all happened so quickly. The next thing I knew, I woke up in the window seat.

VALERIE. So that must be why the window was open.
McKENZIE. What do you mean?

VALERIE. *(Crossing to the window R.)* When I came downstairs, this window was wide open and banging in the wind. I just assumed that the storm had blown it open – but I imagine that whoever put Charles in here must have used the window to escape and left it open behind them.

WILLY. Why would somebody want to thump you over the head and stuff you in the window seat? What were they after?

CHARLES. I can't imagine. What are you all doing down here at this time of night?

WILLY. Holding a Satanic mass.

CHARLES. That explains the candles.

McKENZIE. Actually we were just catching up on our reading. We found the most fascinating book.

*(She holds up the journal.)*

> CHARLES. Where did you find that?
> VALERIE. More to the point, Charles, where did you find it?

*(CHARLES, looking trapped, says nothing.)*

> McKENZIE. You want to tell us what this is all about, Charles?

*(CHARLES opens his mouth to respond, but is interrupted by a loud creaking sound from behind the panel. Everyone is startled by the noise.)*

> WILLY. What was that?
> HENRI. Oh my God!
> McKENZIE. It's coming from the passageway.

*(Another creak.)*

> VALERIE. What on earth could it be?
> McKENZIE. *(Picks up the candle from the coffee table.)* Let's have a look.
> HENRI. Be careful, McKenzie.
> WILLY. Boy, this weekend's turning into a real barrel of laughs, isn't it? Exploding pumpkins, ghosts in the passageway, things that go bump in the night ... all we need now is a body in the closet.

*(McKENZIE opens the secret panel. ELWOOD, covered in blood, is discovered hanging on the inside of it, a hatchet buried in his chest. Gasps all around.)*

CHARLES. Elwood!

*(HENRI faints. McKENZIE screams and drops the candle, extinguishing it as the lights fade to black.)*

END OF ACT I.

## ACT II

### *Scene One*

*(Setting: It is a few minutes later. The storm is raging. ELWOOD is still hanging on the closet door, and HENRI is now sitting on the sofa with VALERIE beside her. A couple of oil lamps have been lit. WILLY is lighting a third one. A fire still burns in the fireplace. CHARLES is crossing down with two glasses of brandy.)*

CHARLES. Are you feeling any better, Henri? You're still awfully pale.

VALERIE. *(Taking a glass from CHARLES and handing it to her.)* Drink this, it'll help.

HENRI. Thank you.

VALERIE. She's alright. It was the shock of finding Elwood hanging there like that.

WILLY. Oh well, it wasn't a total loss. We also found these lamps!

CHARLES. Willy.

*(He crosses to McKENZIE, who is sitting in the armchair in shock.)*

HENRI. Are you all right, McKenzie?

*(CHARLES gives McKENZIE a glass.)*

CHARLES. Here.

McKENZIE. Hmm? Oh, thanks.

*(She downs it in one gulp.)*

HENRI. This is such a nightmare.

WILLY. Oh I don't know. It's not that bad. We've got a cozy little cottage here, *(Gesturing to ELWOOD.)* a few friends hanging around; maybe we could stoke up the fire and roast some marshmallows.

VALERIE. Willy, please. This is no time for levity!

CHARLES. Yes, have a little compassion. Elwood's just been murdered, for God's sake!

WILLY. I'm just trying to lighten the atmosphere a little, that's all.

CHARLES. Well, it's not working.

McKENZIE. So what are we going to do?

WILLY. Well, we could start by closing that door. *(He wheels over to the panel.)* Elwood wasn't much to look at when he was alive; dying sure hasn't improved him.

VALERIE. Shouldn't we take him off that hook? We can't just leave him hanging there.

CHARLES. I don't think that's a good idea. We don't want to tamper with the evidence.

WILLY. Can't we at least close the door?

HENRI. Yes, please. I can't bear him staring at us like that.

CHARLES. Alright.

WILLY. I'll do it.

*(He pulls a handkerchief from his pocket, and carefully closes the door. They all avert their eyes.)*

McKENZIE. *(Hiding her face in her hands.)* Oh God.

HENRI. Oh McKenzie, you poor thing. This must be such a shock for you.

VALERIE. Yes, I'm very sorry for your loss.

CHARLES. Would you like another brandy?

McKENZIE. Yeah, I could use a refill.

*(CHARLES takes her glass, crosses to the drinks table, pours a drink and crosses back with a snifter of brandy.)*

WILLY. So Charles, what do you think we should do?

CHARLES. For the moment there's nothing we can do.

HENRI. Surely there must be some way of contacting the police.

CHARLES. Not until tomorrow. Without a phone we have no way of getting in touch with anyone. Mortie's scheduled to pick us up in the boat tomorrow morning. We'll just have to wait until then.

McKENZIE. We can't just sit here doing nothing. There's got to be a way of getting in touch with someone.

WILLY. Yeah, couldn't we send up a flare or something?

CHARLES. And where would we find one? This isn't an ocean liner.

VALERIE. Maybe we could find another way to get to the mainland.

WILLY. Yeah, most places like this have a canoe or a row boat or something that floats. Maybe we should look around.

CHARLES. You saw where we docked. If there was another boat we would have seen it.

HENRI. How far is the next island? Maybe one of us could try swimming to it.

CHARLES. You'd never survive it. Not in this weather.

McKENZIE. Oh, for God's sake, Charles, do you have to be so negative?

WILLY. Yeah, instead of shooting down everyone else's ideas, maybe you should try coming up with a few of your own.

CHARLES. I'm sorry. If I had any ideas I'd suggest them, believe me. But the fact of the matter is, until that boat comes to pick us up tomorrow, we're on our own.

McKENZIE. Do you honestly expect us to sit here all night with Elwood's body hanging there and a murderer in the room?

*(There is a loud clap of thunder.)*

HENRI. Oh God! You mean one of *us* killed him?

WILLY. Of course, it had to be one of us.

VALERIE. We don't know that for sure. There could be someone else on the island.

WILLY. Come on, Valerie, this island's nothing but bare rock. There's nowhere for anyone to hide.

CHARLES. And no-one knows we're here anyway.

HENRI. Except for that fellow who brought us here in his boat.

WILLY. Why would he want to kill Elwood? No, it has to have been one of us.

VALERIE. The question is, who?

WILLY. Maybe Charles could shed some light on that.

CHARLES. How so?

WILLY. *(Picking up the journal.)* Well, you could start by explaining what this journal is all about.

VALERIE. *(Taking the journal from WILLY.)* Yes, and why you have kept it a secret for so long. Don't you realize how important this information is? We could have used it to find out what happened to Daddy.

CHARLES. Daddy?

WILLY. Yeah, didn't you know? Henri and Valerie's old man was one of the Phantom Five.

CHARLES. What?

WILLY. Hank Addison of Addison Utilities.

CHARLES. Hank Addison was your father? Oh my God! I'm so sorry. I had no idea. Believe me, if I'd known, I never would have brought you here –

VALERIE. You still haven't answered the question. Why haven't you told anyone about the journal?

CHARLES. Because there's nothing to tell. It's a fake.

McKENZIE. A fake?

CHARLES. You didn't really believe it was genuine, did you? Look, ever since the Phantom Five disappeared, people have been coming up with so-called pieces of "evidence" like that journal. They've all been investigated by the authorities, and they've all turned out to be hoaxes.

WILLY. *(To VALERIE and HENRI.)* Is that true?

HENRI. Well, yes, I suppose it is. Stories like our father's tend to bring out a lot of crackpots, I'm afraid.

CHARLES. *(Taking the journal.)* Exactly. And we're right in the middle of it here in Cassandra Lakes. The mystery of the Phantom Five has made it a huge tourist attraction. You can't walk into a store without someone trying to sell you some supposedly authentic artifact connected to the disappearance. The only reason I bothered to pick this book up was because of the games.

WILLY. Well if it's a fake, someone's gone to a lot of trouble to make it look authentic.

CHARLES. To the uneducated eye, perhaps. But I did a little research on the company that makes these notebooks, and you'll be interested to know that they didn't start producing them until a couple of years after the Phantom Five had already disappeared!

WILLY. So it's a hoax.

CHARLES. I'm afraid so. Apparently the author of this book was another proponent of the theory that the Phantom Five were actually the Phantom Six. *(A loud clap of thunder.)* He fabricated this journal to back up his theory – and make a few dollars in the process, I suppose.

HENRI. But people have been speculating for years that there was a sixth person.

CHARLES. And that's precisely what this is. Speculation. I must admit, he's done a credible job. There's some terrific stuff in here. Ah, here's a good bit from the last game ... *(He reads.)* "The unthinkable has happened; The Mousetrap Society has been discovered. We were apparently followed here to Haddington House, and as a result we had to terminate the game immediately. I will, of course, see to it that the member responsible for this catastrophe is disciplined accordingly; however there remains the problem of how best to accommodate our uninvited guest." Excellent stuff, wouldn't you say, Valerie?

VALERIE. Very inventive.

McKENZIE. Boy, sounds like these guys took their privacy seriously.

WILLY. Hey, who knows? Maybe the guy who wrote this journal guessed right – maybe there was a sixth person. That would explain how the rest of them disappeared, wouldn't it? Maybe this uninvited guest followed them here to bump them all off!

CHARLES. Or maybe they were abducted by aliens! *(Holding up journal.)* The point is, this is a work of fiction. And it has nothing to do with Elwood's murder.

WILLY. I'm not so sure of that, Charles.

CHARLES. What do you mean?

WILLY. Well, whether that thing's real or not, it almost looks as though you're trying to get us to act out in real life what's written down in there. First you start up your own version of "The Mousetrap Society", then you get us to play your games every Halloween, and finally you bring us to Haddington House, which, according to the journal, is the very place where the Phantom Five disappeared.

CHARLES. But I've already explained –

WILLY. And no sooner do we arrive here, than we start "disappearing" too. Doesn't that seem like a bit of a coincidence to you?

CHARLES. Are you saying that I brought you here in some perverted attempt to create another Phantom Five?

McKENZIE. Well, if you wanted to make somebody disappear, what better place to do it?

CHARLES. Don't be ridiculous. I have no reason to want Elwood to disappear.

WILLY. Is that so? I take it you got one of these?

*(He takes out his letter and holds it up.)*

CHARLES. Yes.

McKENZIE. It looks as though we all did.

WILLY. Call me crazy, but I figure that Elwood was skewered because of one of these letters. I mean, Elwood picks this weird prize, threatens to blow us away if we don't pay up and suddenly turns up dead. It seems obvious that somebody thought it was better to kill him than to give him what he asked for – and given all the evidence, I think that somebody was you, Charles.

CHARLES. What evidence? All I've heard is supposition. I could just as easily point the finger at you, Willy. You're the one who flew off the handle when Elwood announced what he wanted from us. Under the circumstances, I'd say that's at least as suspicious as anything I've done. If your theory is correct and one of those letters was the reason for Elwood's death, all that tells us is that any one of us could have done it.

VALERIE. So how do we determine who it was?

HENRI. Perhaps we should read them out.

McKENZIE. No way. Forget it.

HENRI. It's the best way of determining who had sufficient motive, wouldn't you agree?

CHARLES. Not necessarily. If we read out the letters, we might only succeed in making everybody look suspicious. In fact we may find ourselves incriminating the wrong person.

HENRI. *(With him.)* – person, yes. I suppose you're right.

CHARLES. Anyway, it's not up to us to determine who murdered Elwood. I say we wait until we get back to the mainland tomorrow and let the police handle it.

VALERIE. Well, this much is certain – once the police become involved, they're going to be very interested in these letters.

WILLY. It's too bad we have to involve the police at all.

HENRI. What?

WILLY. Well when you think about it, whoever killed Elwood did us all a favour.

McKENZIE. What is that supposed to mean?

WILLY. I'm saying that we're all off the hook now. Well, all except Elwood.

CHARLES. Willy! Have a little consideration.

WILLY. Sorry. All I meant was, the rest of us don't have to worry about following through on these favours now, thanks to Elwood's murderer.

HENRI. That's true.

WILLY. A jail sentence seems like a lousy way of paying them back, don't you think?

CHARLES. Perhaps. But that's up to the police, isn't it?

WILLY. Is it?

CHARLES. What are you saying exactly?

WILLY. Why do the police have to find out about it? Thanks to you Charles, nobody knows we're here. We could just keep it to ourselves.

CHARLES. And what do we do about Elwood?

WILLY. We'd have to dispose of the body, of course, but that wouldn't be too difficult. All we'd have to do is put a few rocks in his pants, and heave him into the lake.

VALERIE. Good God!

HENRI. It might work, you know. People do that kind of thing in Raymond Chandler all the time, don't they, Valerie?

VALERIE. Yes, but those books are just fiction. It's not so easy to do it in real life, you know.

WILLY. Oh, come on. How hard could it be? All we have to do is toss him in the lake and tomorrow we all go home and keep our mouths shut. Nobody'll ever know what happened to him.

McKENZIE. I can't believe you'd even suggest such a thing, Willy.

WILLY. Hey, look. I'm just thinking of those of us who are innocent. I mean, only one of us killed him, right? Why should the rest of us have to have the cops breathing down our necks?

CHARLES. Forget it, Willy. All moral considerations aside, your plan would never work. There *is* someone who knows where we are – Mortie. When he comes to pick us up in the boat tomorrow, how do we explain to him why Elwood's not with us? No matter what we tell him, once Elwood's been reported missing, Mortie's going to tell the police what he knows. We'll be the first ones they'll want to question.

WILLY. I didn't think of that.

VALERIE. We may not be able to dispose of Elwood, but there's nothing to stop us from disposing of the letters.

*(Beat. They all look at each other.)*

HENRI. Pardon?

CHARLES. What do you mean?

VALERIE. Well, as Willy said, there's no reason why those of us who didn't kill Elwood should have our private business made public. If we allow the police to see those letters, it'll only be a matter of time before the media get hold of them.

HENRI. The media? Oh God.

VALERIE. Yes, and you know what those vultures are like. I say we get rid of those letters as soon as possible.

WILLY. She's got a point, Charles.

HENRI. *(With him.)* – point, Charles, yes.

CHARLES. But you realize that if we do that, we'll all be guilty of destroying evidence – evidence that could lead to Elwood's killer.

WILLY. Personally, I could live with that.

VALERIE. So what do you say, Charles? Shall we do it?

CHARLES. I really thing you're asking the wrong person. How do you feel about this, McKenzie?

*(Beat)*

McKENZIE. Well, if our only other choice is to make them public, I say burn the damn things.

*(Everyone looks at McKENZIE. She calmly sips her drink.)*

CHARLES. *(Slightly taken aback.)* Alright, if that's what everyone wants ...

WILLY. Yeah, yeah, let's do it.

CHARLES. Very well, let's have them then. I'll throw them in the fire. McKenzie?

McKENZIE. *(Pulling her letter out of her pocket.)* Here you go – and good riddance to it.

CHARLES. I almost regret having to do this. I'm sure they'd make for some fascinating reading. *(Turning to HENRI and VALERIE.)* Ladies?

VALERIE. Here you are.

HENRI. *(With her.)* – you are, Charles.

CHARLES. *(Taking their letters and turning to WILLY.)* Thank you. And yours.

WILLY. Right here.

CHARLES. Thank you. That just leaves mine. *(Reaching into his inside jacket pocket, then trying the other pockets.)* Wait a minute. Where has it gone?

*(There is a crack of thunder. The door of the panel suddenly swings open to reveal ELWOOD still hanging on the inside. They all jump.)*

McKENZIE. Elwood!

VALERIE. Oh my God!

WILLY. How did that happen?

HENRI. This place is haunted, I keep telling you!

WILLY. *(Wheeling over to the panel door.)* Don't panic. It's alright. It was probably just the catch on the door giving way, or something. Just a second – look at this!

CHARLES. What is it?

WILLY. Looks like Elwood has something he wants to get off his chest.

McKENZIE. What?

WILLY. There's a note attached to him. *(Pointing to ELWOOD.)* Look.

*(He pulls the pin from ELWOOD's chest and removes the note. He looks at the pin, looks at ELWOOD, then sticks the pin back into ELWOOD's chest and begins to read the note.)*

VALERIE. How did that get there?

HENRI. I dread to think.

McKENZIE. Never a dull moment around this place, is there?

CHARLES. *(Closing the door.)* Well Willy, what does it say?

WILLY. Hold on.

McKENZIE. Hurry up. The suspense is killing me.

*(WILLY looks at CHARLES and then back to the letter.)*

WILLY. Well, Charles. You said you had no reason for wanting Elwood dead. Looks like we've just been provided with one.

HENRI. What is it?

WILLY. It's Charles' letter.

CHARLES. I'd appreciate it if you would give that back to me, Willy.

WILLY. It's too late Charles.

CHARLES. We just agreed to destroy those letters!

WILLY. Yeah, but in light of the fact that yours just showed up stuck to a dead body, I'd say the situation has changed.

CHARLES. *(Crossing to WILLY.)* Give it back!

WILLY. *(Holding the letter out to him.)* Fine, if that's what you want. But I've already read it, remember.

*(CHARLES stops.)*

McKENZIE. What does it say, Willy?

WILLY. Do you want to read it out, or shall I? *(CHARLES turns and walks away in defeat.)* "Dear Charles, I've had a look at your new manuscript, 'Robbed Blind', and it's pretty clear who your antagonist is intended to be. I have no idea how you got your information, but I'm sure you'll understand that I cannot allow this book to be released. My request to you is that you stop its publication and destroy any material pertaining to it – including this letter, of course. Yours Truly, Elwood O'Callaghan."

HENRI. What was your book about, Charles?

CHARLES. It was loosely based on the Woolford Corporation scandal.

WILLY. Oh yeah, the insider trading thing.

VALERIE. Who is it that Elwood thought you had exposed?

CHARLES. Well, in my novel the villain is a rich, powerful businessman who owns a large number of companies.

McKENZIE. A hundred and forty-seven of them, maybe?

CHARLES. Something like that.

WILLY. How did you find out that Elwood was mixed up in the Woolford case?

CHARLES. I didn't! That's the irony. It was totally accidental. I just made it up!

McKENZIE. That's unbelievable.

CHARLES. Maybe so, but it's the truth. Look, if I'd known Elwood was involved in the Woolford scandal, do you think I would have set out to expose him like this? I'm not entirely stupid. The book is a work of fiction.

McKENZIE. And any resemblance to persons living or dead is purely coincidental, right?

WILLY. It doesn't matter though, does it? Elwood believed that if the book got published, he'd be hung out to dry.

CHARLES. So it seems.

McKENZIE. How much is a book deal like this worth to you, Charles?

CHARLES. Including paperback, film and foreign language rights, a conservative estimate would be something close to six million dollars.

*(Gasps all around.)*

WILLY. That's a nice chunk of change.

CHARLES. Of course, I've already received a million of that as an advance. Which I've spent.

McKENZIE. Sounds like you had a hell of a good motive for killing him.

CHARLES. Yes, I can't deny that. Money is certainly one of the most common motives for murder.

WILLY. You trying to tell us you did it?

CHARLES. Don't be absurd. I'm simply saying that on the surface, it would appear I had good reason to. But I didn't kill him.

VALERIE. Have you any way of proving that?

CHARLES. As a matter of fact, I do. If you'll recall, I was lying unconscious in the window seat when he was murdered.

HENRI. We don't know that. You could have climbed in the window seat after you'd hung him up in there.

CHARLES. But why would I do that? Why not escape out the window?

WILLY. Much better to let us discover you in the window seat, supposedly unconscious. That way, you've got an alibi.

CHARLES. And how do you explain this bump on my head? Are you suggesting that I did that to myself too?

McKENZIE. Not necessarily. Maybe Elwood gave it to you in the struggle, before you managed to subdue him.

CHARLES. *(Finding himself at the mantelpiece, he opens the humidor.)* You've all read too many of my books. Look, if I killed Elwood, why would I advertise the fact by sticking my letter on his body? I think it's much more likely that the real murderer put my letter there in an attempt to frame me.

WILLY. Well, they're doing a helluva good job.

CHARLES. Listen, we all got letters. For all I know, each one of you could have just as good a motive for killing Elwood as I have. I say we read them all out.

VALERIE. Absolutely not! We agreed to get rid of them.

CHARLES. Yes, but that was before someone decided to use my letter to try and make me out to be a murderer. Look, what if you're wrong? What if it wasn't me? If you destroy these letters, you may also destroy the only chance you have of finding the real culprit.

WILLY. Come on, Charles, hand them over!

CHARLES. Over my dead body.

*(He turns to the mantel and quickly turns back with a gun in his hand.)*

HENRI. He's got a gun!

VALERIE. Don't shoot!

WILLY. Take it easy, Charles!

CHARLES. No need to panic. I'm just having a smoke.

*(He holds up a cigar in his other hand and lights it with the gun/lighter, and replaces it on the mantel. He takes a puff, licks his lips.)*

WILLY. Why can't you use matches, like everybody else?

McKENZIE. Yeah, for a moment there I thought you were about to kill the rest of us off.

CHARLES. I think we've had enough murders for one night, don't you? *(Puffing on the cigar.)* Hmm. Tastes a bit stale.

*(He takes another puff and starts to cough.)*

VALERIE. I wish you wouldn't smoke those, Charles, I really can't take the smell. *(CHARLES coughs more heavily.)* Charles?

McKENZIE. Charles? Are you alright?

*(CHARLES tries to answer but cannot. He stumbles forward and falls to his knees, gasping for breath.)*

WILLY. Charles!

HENRI. *(Kneeling next to him.)* Oh my god!

VALERIE. Somebody do something!

*(CHARLES collapses, gulping for air, finally losing consciousness.)*

HENRI. *(Shaking him.)* Charles!!! *(She shakes him again, there is no response. She puts her head on his chest, listens for a heartbeat.)* He's dead.

*(She gently closes his eyes.)*

McKENZIE. Oh my god! What do you think it was, a heart attack?

*(WILLY takes the cigar out of CHARLES' hand and sniffs it.)*

WILLY. Smells like almonds.
VALERIE. *(Taking the cigar and smelling it.)* Cyanide. He's been murdered.

*(Blackout)*

### *Scene Two*

*(The same. About ten minutes later. The storm is almost at an end. There are occasional flashes of lightning and rumbles of thunder in the distance. CHARLES' body is gone. WILLY is on stage alone, with the pile of letters [sans envelopes] on his lap. He is reading one of them. He finishes the letter, folds it up, and puts all of them into his inner pocket. Suddenly the panel door flies open with ELWOOD hanging on the inside of it. WILLY starts.)*

WILLY. Jeez Louise! *(Wheeling himself over to the panel.)* What's the matter, Elwood? Feeling left out? *(As he reaches the panel.)* Won't be much longer now, pal. Hang in there.

*(He closes the door just as HENRI and McKENZIE enter from UR.)*

McKENZIE. We put him on the bed, Willy.
WILLY. Did you have to use my room? I'm not sure I like the idea of sharing my bed with a corpse.

McKENZIE. Well it's the best we could do. You didn't expect us to cart him up the stairs, did you?

WILLY. You could have put him back in the window seat.

HENRI. Where's Valerie?

WILLY. She went outside.

HENRI. What?

WILLY. She's still not convinced we're the only ones on the island. She wants to see for herself that no-one's lurking around out there.

McKENZIE. You let her go out by herself?

WILLY. Don't worry, she can't go anywhere.

McKENZIE. What do you think she's doing

WILLY. I don't know. Checking for footprints, maybe?

HENRI. I don't like the idea of her being out there alone. It's too dangerous.

WILLY. Relax, will you?

*(The front door opens and VALERIE enters, dressed in raincoat, hat and boots and carrying the flashlight. Now that another murder has occurred, the remaining members of the group are considerably more suspicious of one another.)*

VALERIE. Goodness, it's cold out there!

WILLY. Not much better in here. *(Wheels over to the fireplace, picks up the poker and starts to poke up the fire.)* So did you see anything, Valerie?

VALERIE. *(Taking off the coat, hat and boots.)* Nothing. You were right. There's no one out there.

McKENZIE. So what do we do now? Sit here with our backs to the wall and stare at each other until the boat arrives?

HENRI. That's not a bad idea, actually. At least if we stay together, we can make sure the killer doesn't strike again.

WILLY. Oh yeah? Tell that to Charles. *(Seeing something in the fire.)* What the hell is this? Hey McKenzie, give me a hand here.

McKENZIE. *(Crossing to him.)* What is it?

WILLY. I'm not sure. Can you reach it?

McKENZIE. I think so. *(Picking up a cloth and reaching into the fire, she pulls out the charred remains of the journal.)* Oh my God.

HENRI. What have you found?
McKENZIE. It's the journal – or what's left of it.
HENRI. Oh no! You mean someone's destroyed it?
WILLY. Yup.
McKENZIE. Who?

*(Beat. They all regard one another suspiciously.)*

VALERIE. But why would anyone bother?
HENRI. *(With her.)* – bother, yes? Didn't Charles say it was a fake?
WILLY. Looks like he was wrong about that. It must have been real. I mean, why else would someone go to the trouble of burning it?
HENRI. But if the journal was real, that means this *is* the place where the Phantom Five disappeared!
McKENZIE. Looks like history is repeating itself after all.
HENRI. You mean we're all going to disappear too?
McKENZIE. Sure looks that way.
VALERIE. But why? I can understand why Elwood was killed, but Charles and the rest of us ... it just doesn't make any sense.
WILLY. Unless the killer is trying to eliminate the witnesses.
McKENZIE. Great. So what do you suggest we do – go and hide in our beds?
WILLY. Not in mine, thanks. It's occupied.
HENRI. Oh my God. We're all going to die.
WILLY. No. We're not going to die. We're going to figure out which one of us is doing this.
VALERIE. Good idea.
HENRI. And how do we do that?
McKENZIE. We should be asking you that question, Henri. You and Valerie are the only ones here with any direct link to the Phantom Five.
WILLY. Yeah, good point. I mean, the rest of us have been playing these games for years without any fatalities. Then you show up and suddenly we start dropping like flies.
VALERIE. But that's ludicrous! We had no idea that Charles was bringing us to Haddington House. And we had no idea that there was

any connection between Haddington House and our father's disappearance. Believe me, if I'd known this is where we were going to end up, I never would have come.

HENRI. *(With her.)* – come, that's for sure. And you could just as easily argue that our connection to this place proves our innocence. It seems obvious to me that someone is trying to make victims of Valerie and me, the same way they did with Daddy.

VALERIE. Exactly.

WILLY. Well, Elwood was trying to make victims of you, wasn't he? He was all set to ruin your good name and take over your business.

VALERIE. How on earth did you know that?

HENRI. *(With her.)* – know that? Yes, Willy.

WILLY. *(Pulling out the letters and holding them up.)* Sorry, I couldn't help myself.

HENRI. You read our letters?

WILLY. Yup.

VALERIE. You were supposed to burn those!

WILLY. So sue me.

McKENZIE. You son of a bitch!

WILLY. Hey, take it easy. I'm not going to sell them to the National Enquirer or anything – look, the only way we're going to crack this thing is to put all our cards on the table.

HENRI. You mean read out the letters?

WILLY. Yes.

McKENZIE. But those letters are private –

WILLY. For God's sake, our lives are at stake here. This is no time to get uptight about privacy!

*(Beat)*

McKENZIE. Yeah, I suppose you're right.

HENRI. Maybe so. What do you think, Valerie?

VALERIE. What difference does it make? The damage has already been done.

HENRI. *(With her.)* – been done, yes. Well Willy, as you've already let the cat halfway out of the bag, we may as well finish the story. *(To McKENZIE.)* Elwood found out that I had been covering up a toxic waste scandal at our plant. He wanted us to go public with the story, which would have bankrupted us. Then he was going to buy Addison Utilities for a pittance.

McKENZIE. No kidding. What does the letter say exactly?

WILLY. *(Giving McKENZIE the letter.)* Here, read it for yourself.

HENRI. I had it taken care of. It was being cleaned up.

VALERIE. I knew nothing about this, by the way. It was all Henriette's doing.

McKENZIE. *(Glancing through the letter.)* Oh I get it. Once the news got out, your stock would drop and Elwood could buy it at a bargain price.

VALERIE. Yes, and in the process he'd be stealing our family business out from under us.

HENRI. *(With her.)* – under us, yes.

McKENZIE. Sounds like Elwood alright. Find a weakness and take advantage of it.

VALERIE. And even if we'd managed to hang on to the business, our reputations would have been destroyed.

McKENZIE. Well, this would definitely be worth killing somebody for.

VALERIE. Perhaps. But I wouldn't be too hasty in your judgments. We did that with Charles, and look where that got us. Remember we still have two letters to read. Let's hear yours, McKenzie.

*(WILLY holds out the letter. She snatches it out of his hand.)*

McKENZIE. *(Reading)* "My Darling: If anyone had told me when I first met you through that escort service that I would find myself in this position some day, I would have laughed at them. I have almost everything that life can offer; but the one thing that has always eluded my grasp is the one thing you have to give me. My request to you, my most cherished possession, is that you make my world complete by agreeing to become my wife. Yours always, Elwood."

*(A beat. McKENZIE folds up the letter and puts it back in the envelope.)*

WILLY. Escort service? Come on, Mack, fess up. You were a hooker.

*(She looks away.)*

HENRI. Good Lord.

VALERIE. Well, now it's clear why you wouldn't want anyone to see that letter.

HENRI. But I don't understand – Elwood wanted to marry you?

McKENZIE. That's what he said, isn't it?

VALERIE. I gather, however, that you didn't want to marry Elwood.

McKENZIE. No. But you know what he was going to do if we didn't give him what he wanted.

HENRI. *(To McKENZIE.)* You mean that if you refused to marry Elwood, he would have killed you?

McKENZIE. That's right.

WILLY. Talk about a shotgun wedding.

HENRI. I still don't understand. It seems a little excessive.

McKENZIE. *(Crossing to drinks table and pouring a drink.)* Not if you know the history.

HENRI. What do you mean? It seemed like Elwood was crazy about you.

McKENZIE. Oh he was crazy, alright. Or maybe obsessed would be a better word for it.

VALERIE. Obsessed?

McKENZIE. *(Raises the glass to her lips, looks at the others suspiciously, puts the glass down.)* My relationship with Elwood was – complicated.

HENRI. In what way?

McKENZIE. Elwood wasn't so much interested in having a relationship with me as he was in having me, period. To him, I was like one of his companies – just another thing to be acquired. Once he decided he wanted me, there was nothing to discuss. My feelings in the matter didn't count.

VALERIE. Well if that's how you felt, why didn't you leave him?

McKENZIE. Oh I tried, a number of times. Kept waking up in the hospital.

HENRI. He beat you?

McKENZIE. Of course.

HENRI. My God.

McKENZIE. Hey, it wasn't a total disaster. I got a new nose out of the deal.

HENRI. How awful.

VALERIE. But I thought you were a very successful model, surely you had the means to get away from him.

McKENZIE. No. He controlled my finances, too. The truth was I couldn't afford to leave him. God knows I wanted to. It wasn't just the beatings. He threatened me, he had me followed everywhere I went, he cut me off from the few friends I had. I was at his mercy. If I had married him I would have been his prisoner for life.

VALERIE. Well, of all the reasons to kill Elwood, yours is certainly the most original. I've never heard of a marriage proposal being a motive for murder before.

McKENZIE. Yeah, well, don't get too excited. We haven't finished yet, have we, Willy?

WILLY. Alright, but before I read this, I want to explain a couple of things.

McKENZIE. Don't try and wriggle out of it. Just read the damn thing.

WILLY. Okay, okay. *(Pulling out a letter and reading.)* "Yaskovitch: – If there's one thing I can't stand, it's people who leave a job unfinished – especially when they've been paid in advance. Fortunately, this game has provided you with a way to make things up to me. My request to you is that you dispose of our friend in Detroit, as previously agreed. I realize this will be somewhat of a challenge, given your disability; but there is, after all, more than one way to skin a cat. Yours Truly, O'Callaghan."

HENRI. He wanted you to kill this man?

*(WILLY nods.)*

VALERIE. Good God. You said you worked for Elwood, but you never mentioned anything about killing for him.

WILLY. I never killed anyone for Elwood. That's the point. Look, I owed the guy. After my football career fell apart, he was the only one who would give me a job. He dried me out, got me back in shape and put me on the payroll as one of his bodyguards. But when he started asking me to do his dirty work for him I just couldn't take it. I tried to get out but, just like McKenzie, he wouldn't let me go. The order to kill the guy in Detroit was the final straw. I knew I couldn't do it, and I knew Elwood would get somebody to take care of me if I didn't. I was desperate to find a way to escape. And then it came to me – if I really *couldn't* do it, if I was physically incapable, he'd have to find somebody else.

HENRI. So you crippled yourself on purpose?

WILLY. Not exactly. I faked it.

*(He stands up. Gasps of surprise from everyone.)*

VALERIE. Willy!

McKENZIE. I don't believe it!

VALERIE. This is astounding! You've been keeping this up for six months?

HENRI. *(With her.)* – months? It's remarkable.

WILLY. I hope I've made my point. I was willing to live the rest of my life like that if it would keep Elwood off my back.

HENRI. But why didn't you tell us right after Elwood was murdered? You had no reason to deceive us any longer.

WILLY. Are you kidding? If I'd hopped out of my chair at that point, you'd all have been convinced that I'd done it.

VALERIE. I'm half-way convinced as it is.

*(WILLY wheels his chair into a corner, out of the way.)*

McKENZIE. *(Watching WILLY.)* And you let Henri and me lug Charles' body into your room? You bastard!

VALERIE. Well I'm sorry Willy, but as far as I'm concerned, your story just makes you look even more guilty.

WILLY. Weren't you listening? The whole reason I went to such extremes, as you put it, is because I couldn't kill anyone. Not even Elwood.

HENRI. You expect us to believe that – a man who made his living as a bodyguard?

WILLY. Hey, aren't you forgetting something? I was the last one in here. Elwood must have been long dead by the time I showed up.

VALERIE. So? You could have killed Elwood before the rest of us came down. You had plenty of time to escape through the window, get back to your room and into your wheelchair.

WILLY. How? The only way back into this place is through the front door. I couldn't have got back into my room without being seen.

VALERIE. You could have crawled in your bedroom window.

WILLY. Impossible. The only window in this place that isn't shuttered is this one, remember? If I'd gone out of the window there would have been no way for me to get back in.

HENRI. That's true. This was the only window Charles opened.

WILLY. So how did I get back to my room? I may be able to walk, but I certainly can't fly.

HENRI. *(With him.)* – fly, no.

WILLY. I'll tell you what I'd like to know – what were the rest of you up to before I came in? I mean, what brought you down here to begin with, Valerie?

VALERIE. As I told you before. I came down to close this window. *(She crosses to the window and pulls open the curtains. The storm has subsided and light is beginning to dawn.)* It was making quite a racket – banging against the side of the house. I had to lean all the way out to get a hold of it. When I came back in Henri was standing right here.

McKENZIE. Well that's your story, anyway.

VALERIE. It's the truth. You didn't see me in here when you came downstairs, did you? And you were obviously down here before I was.

WILLY. She was?

VALERIE. Yes, she was in there, having a bath.

WILLY. A bath? Why would you want to take a bath in the middle of the night?

McKENZIE. I was trying to get warm.

VALERIE. Or clean. The bathroom would be the perfect place to hide if you were covered in blood.

McKNEZIE. What are you saying?

VALERIE. Well, you could have murdered Elwood, then dealt with Charles; and when you heard me coming downstairs, you jumped out the window. Then you could have crawled in the bathroom window, cleaned yourself up and come in here a few minutes later.

HENRI. *(With her.)* – minutes later, yes.

McKENZIE. Nice try, Valerie, but as Willy just said, the bathroom window is shuttered – not to mention the fact that I didn't read my letter until I came in here and found it – you and Henri were witnesses to that. Elwood was already dead by then. So when he was murdered I had no motive for killing him.

HENRI. That's true, Valerie.

VALERIE. So where does that leave us?

WILLY. In pretty good shape, actually. We've managed to eliminate everybody.

McKENZIE. No we haven't. There's still one person whose movements we haven't accounted for.

HENRI. Who?

McKENZIE. You, Henri.

HENRI. We certainly have. I told you, I came downstairs just after Valerie.

McKENZIE. Yes, but where were you before she came downstairs?

VALERIE. She was asleep in our room.

WILLY. How do you know?

VALERIE. Because I was wide awake the whole time. After I read Elwood's letter I couldn't sleep a wink. When I went down to investigate what that noise was, Henri was still in her bed.

McKENZIE. So you say.

VALERIE. What do you mean? I saw her lying there.

McKENZIE. Either that or you're covering up for her.

VALERIE. What are you implying, McKenzie?

McKENZIE. That the two of you killed Elwood together.

VALERIE. That's nonsense!

HENRI. *(With her.)* – nonsense!

McKENZIE. I don't know. It makes sense to me. Maybe it happened something like this: you and Henri cooked up the idea of killing Elwood after you'd read your letter. When you heard him coming downstairs to plant my letter you followed him. One of you got him talking, probably about his request, while the other one grabbed the hatchet and killed him. You stuck him up there on the door and used the passageway to sneak back up to your room.

VALERIE. But that's ridiculous. The only reason I came downstairs was because that window was open and banging in the wind.

McKENZIE. Oh the window was open, alright. But that happened after you'd gone back upstairs. Maybe you thought it was Elwood – that he wasn't quite dead. So you came down, opened the panel to check on him when suddenly Charles showed up. You knocked him out and stuck him in the window seat.

VALERIE. It doesn't follow. If we were the cold-blooded murderers you claim we are, why would we only knock Charles out? Why wouldn't we just kill him and be done with it?

WILLY. Maybe you thought you had killed him. And when he woke up you realized you'd have to come up with another way of doing it.

McKENZIE. Right. So you poisoned his cigars. And once he was out of the way, all you had to do was kill Willy and me and you'd be free and clear.

HENRI. That's an interesting theory you've come up with. There's only one problem with it. It's a little too close to the truth.

*(She pulls a gun out of her pocket and levels it at WILLY.)*

WILLY. Henri!
McKENZIE. What are you doing?

*(HENRI shoots WILLY, McKENZIE screams. HENRI points the gun at McKENZIE and shoots her. WILLY and McKENZIE crumple to the floor.)*

VALERIE. Henriette!!!
HENRI. *(Crossing to the bodies to make sure they're dead.)* Shut up!
VALERIE. What in God's name are you doing?
HENRI. Finishing what I started.
VALERIE. *(Suddenly realizing.) You* killed Elwood?

HENRI. And Charles. McKenzie was right, for the most part. She just got the timing wrong.

VALERIE. You couldn't have. You were asleep beside me all night.

HENRI. That's true. But I killed Elwood before I even went to bed – while he was planting McKenzie's letter. I was just cleaning up when Charles came down. It seemed as good a time as any to take care of him as well. Obviously I didn't hit him hard enough. Then I went upstairs, took Elwood's gun from his room, and went to bed. The storm must have blown the window open, just as you first thought. When you came down to close it, Elwood had already been dead for a couple of hours.

VALERIE. But why did you kill Charles?

*(HENRI turns to VALERIE, pointing the gun.)*

HENRI. The same reason I killed the others.

VALERIE. And now you're going to kill me too?

HENRI. Not exactly. You're going to commit suicide.

VALERIE. Suicide?

HENRI. Yes. You've been behaving very strangely lately – talking more and more about death – even contemplating killing yourself. I was getting quite worried about you, and was careful to express my concern to a number of people. I thought coming away this weekend might help to cheer you up. Unfortunately the plan backfired with tragic results. Something caused you to snap. You killed the others and would have killed me too, if I hadn't managed to escape. Finally you turned the gun on yourself.

VALERIE. You're deranged! No-one's going to believe a story like that.

HENRI. Why shouldn't they? There won't be anyone around to contradict me, will there?

VALERIE. This is crazy! Why would I want to kill a group of people I barely know?

HENRI. Why not? You've done it before – Julia.

VALERIE. What did you call me?

HENRI. There's no point in pretending anymore, Julia. I know who you are.

VALERIE. I don't know what you're talking about.

HENRI. Of course you do. Julia Boothman. The uninvited guest from The Mousetrap Society's final game. *(Beat. HENRI pulls out a worn photograph and shows it to VALERIE.)* Have another look at this photograph. Good thing I had the presence of mind to remove it from the journal before you threw it in the fire. Recognize anything?

VALERIE. It's Haddington House. So what?

HENRI. Look a little closer. Someone was coming through the front door just as the picture was being taken. See how she's looking off toward the horizon? She had no idea that the photographer had caught her.

VALERIE. *(Looking at the picture.)* Oh my God, it's me!

HENRI. Twenty-five years ago.

VALERIE. So that's what this whole weekend has been about. I knew something was up from the minute I saw where we were. I just couldn't figure out who was behind it.

HENRI. I was counting on that. I thought I would be the last person you'd suspect.

VALERIE. So this has all been your twisted attempt at wreaking revenge.

HENRI. What do you expect? You killed my father.

VALERIE. And you killed four innocent people.

HENRI. No, Julia. *I* didn't kill anyone. You did – and then you killed yourself. At least, that's what the world is going to believe.

VALERIE. Well, if you're going to kill me, let's get on with it.

HENRI. Not yet. First you've got a little explaining to do.

VALERIE. Find your own answers.

*(VALERIE darts to the fireplace and tosses the photo into the fire.)*

HENRI. Stop! *(She fires the gun and hits a plate on the mantel above VALERIE's head. The plate smashes. HENRI points the gun at VALERIE.)* Sit down!

VALERIE. Alright, alright. *(She crosses calmly to the sofa and sits.)* My goodness, I didn't know you had it in you. Well, you were right about one thing, Henri. I'd never have guessed you were on to me.

HENRI. I wasn't, for a long time. For twenty-five years you had me believing you were my sister.

VALERIE. I am, legally speaking. Your father adopted me.

HENRI. And how did you get him to do that?

VALERIE. Easy. I got him to fall in love with me.

HENRI. Why?

VALERIE. For the money, Henri, why else?

HENRI. Go on.

VALERIE. I wish you'd put that thing down. This is difficult enough without a gun staring me in the face. *(HENRI cocks the gun.)* Alright! *(Beat. She stares at HENRI and then begins to speak – coldly, slightly amused by it all.)* Your father and I were having an affair. But I was only seventeen at the time, and your father was terrified that someone would find out about us. I came up with a great solution to the problem – he could adopt me. That way I could move right into the house. He convinced your mother I was the orphaned daughter of some distant relative, that he felt duty-bound to take me in. She believed it. So he had the adoption papers drawn up, had my name legally changed, and I became your sister.

HENRI. I don't believe it!

VALERIE. Oh, it was a piece of cake. Your mother took a real shine to me. There was only one problem: the will. As it stood, everything was left to her. She'd been bedridden ever since she'd given birth to you two years before, but she didn't seem to be in any hurry to hop the twig. She could have lived for decades. I didn't want to wait, so I decided to help her along.

HENRI. Help her along? But mother's death was accidental.

VALERIE. She was taking so many prescriptions, she was single-handedly keeping the local pharmacy in business. It wasn't hard to arrange an overdose.

HENRI. You killed my mother?

VALERIE. Technically your father did. He's the one who fed her the pills. Of course, he didn't realize I'd switched the bottles around.

HENRI. What kind of a monster are you?

VALERIE. I'd say that's a case of the pot calling the kettle noir, wouldn't you, Henriette? Anyway, soon after she died I pointed out to Hank that should anything happen to him, he would need someone to look after you – you were only a baby, after all. He didn't think twice. He made me your guardian and divided the estate between us.

HENRI. So you had everything you wanted. Why did you kill him?

VALERIE. Shortly after he changed the will, things began to deteriorate between us. I think he suspected what had really happened to your mother. Things finally came to a head just before Halloween. He was preparing to go away for the weekend. We had a huge fight, in the midst of which he told me to get out – that it was over – that he was going to cut me out of the will. He said that when he got back on Monday, he expected me to have my bags packed. I was about to lose everything I'd worked for. So when he left I followed him.

HENRI. All the way to Haddington House.

VALERIE. That's right. It wasn't easy, let me tell you. *(Laughing)* They were all furious when they saw me. This Mousetrap Society was apparently such a well-kept secret that no one else in the world knew where they were. When I heard that, I knew what I was going to do.

HENRI. And you killed him?

VALERIE. I had to. Killing your father was the only way to make sure that my share of the estate was safe.

HENRI. And the rest of the Phantom Five?

VALERIE. I killed them all. Colin Jeffries, Mara English, Don Ewes and Ronald Roberts.

HENRI. But why?

VALERIE. For the same reason you killed everyone here, I expect; to eliminate the witnesses. Once the bodies were disposed of, no-one would ever be able to connect me to their disappearance.

HENRI. And where was I during all of this?

VALERIE. *(Smugly)* Right here, actually. I'd brought you with me.

HENRI. What?

VALERIE. While I was taking care of the others, you were fast asleep in Willy's room.

HENRI. I was here? Oh my God!

VALERIE. A few days later I reported "Daddy" was missing. Soon after, the press got hold of the story, dubbed it "The Phantom

Five" and turned it into another Bermuda Triangle. It never occurred to anyone to consider me as a suspect. I was just another one of the grieving relatives.

HENRI. You had your share of the estate. Why didn't you just take the money and run?

VALERIE. I couldn't. It took seven years before they would even declare your father dead. Then I had to wait for the will to clear probate. By the time it did, I was already running the company.

HENRI. So for twenty-five years you got away with it.

VALERIE. Yes. And if it hadn't been for that journal, no-one would ever have found out.

HENRI. *(Sinking into the sofa beside VALERIE.)* And all these years you let me believe ...

VALERIE. *(Laughing softly to herself.)* There's a lovely irony to all of this, you know. For so many years I believed you and I were such complete opposites. Turns our we're not so different after all. *(HENRI turns slightly, the gun lowered. VALERIE puts a comforting arm around HENRI's shoulder, then suddenly grabs the gun and wrests it from HENRI's grasp.)* I'll take that, thank you very much. *(She gets up, pointing the gun at HENRI. HENRI stands and begins to back away slowly.)* Well. It looks as though history is repeating itself after all. The only difference is this time *I* shall have to disappear too. Still, that shouldn't be hard – not with the Addison fortune at my disposal. Not exactly the finale you had in mind, is it Henriette? Ah well, the best laid plans ... Goodbye, Little Sister. *(She shoots HENRI. HENRI just smiles at her.)* What the hell ... ?

*(She takes aim and shoots again.)*

HENRI. Go ahead, Julia, try it again. *(VALERIE shoots the last bullet, followed by a series of clicks as she tries in vain to blow HENRI away.)* You don't think I'd be so stupid as to let you get hold of a loaded gun, do you?

*(With a wail of frustration, VALERIE throws the gun down on the chair and launches herself upon HENRI. She starts to choke her. As they struggle, the secret panel flies open and ELWOOD, the hatchet still sticking out of his chest, steps out. VALERIE screams.)*

VALERIE. Elwood! *(He takes a step towards her. She screams again, turns and runs towards the main entrance at which point CHARLES enters through the archway, smoking his cigar. She screams again, and turns to see WILLY and McKENZIE getting up from the floor.)* What the ... ?

*(She backs up to the bookcase UC.)*

CHARLES. Well done, Henri.

VALERIE. What's going on?

CHARLES. I hope you'll excuse the amateur theatricals, Julia, but they were a necessary evil.

*(ELWOOD removes the hatchet from his chest; the others begin to wipe off blood, etc.)*

VALERIE. *(The penny drops.)* Oh my God. You mean this whole thing was a scam?

HENRI. Of course.

VALERIE. I don't understand. You did all this to make me think Henri was a murderer? Why?

McKENZIE. We had to make you believe that story, in order to get you to talk.

VALERIE. Who are you people?

CHARLES. Allow me to introduce you. Julia Boothman, may I present Elwood Jeffries, McKenzie Roberts and Willy English.

VALERIE. Jeffries, Roberts – you mean ... ?

ELWOOD. That's right. We're the relatives of those people you murdered – The Phantom Five.

CHARLES. It was a risk, of course, bringing you to Haddington House. We knew that the moment you saw where you were, you could have refused to go along with our game. In that event we were prepared to force a confession out of you, but fortunately you decided to be a good sport.

VALERIE. You can't prove a thing, you know.

CHARLES. *(Crossing to the coffee table, and reaches underneath it.)* Can't we?

VALERIE. You don't have any physical evidence. I burned the journal – and that photograph.

CHARLES. But you confessed.

VALERIE. Your word against mine. You don't have a thing that'd stand up in court.

*(From under the table, CHARLES pulls out the same tape recorder as in Act One.)*

CHARLES. Let's see about that, shall we?

*(He pushes a button and we hear the following played back:)*

HENRI's VOICE. And the rest of the Phantom Five?

VALERIE's VOICE. I killed them all. Colin Jeffries, Mara English, Don Ewes and Ronald Roberts.

*(CHARLES stops the tape, takes the cassette out. VALERIE, defeated, collapses into a chair.)*

VALERIE. *(To HENRI.)* How did you find out who I was?

HENRI. Oh that was Charles' discovery.

CHARLES. Yes, I've been researching the Phantom Five disappearance for years. I wanted to base my next novel on it. Despite all the theories about how they disappeared, I've always been convinced that it was murder. So, I did what any self-respecting murder investigator would do – I followed the money. You were one of a number of people who benefitted from the disappearance, but when I found that photograph in the journal I knew that the sixth person had to be a young woman. You were the only person on the list who fit that description. I contacted Henri and showed her the photograph. She identified you immediately.

VALERIE. Where did you find that journal to begin with?

CHARLES. Exactly where McKenzie did. About a year ago, I was looking at several locations in this area as possible sites for the disappearance. Haddington House was just one of them. I was going through the bookshelves when I stumbled across the journal in its secret compartment. Of course, that nonsense about it being a fake was all part of our story. It was real enough, as you must have known.

VALERIE. Indeed. So if you knew it was me, why didn't you go to the police?

HENRI. We did. They told us we didn't have a case. There was no way of proving that the journal was authentic, and they wouldn't accept a twenty-five year old Polaroid as positive identification. In any event, it was impossible to prove exactly when that picture had been taken.

CHARLES. So, as compelling as this evidence was, it wasn't enough. If we wanted to have you arrested we needed to get a confession. That's when we decided to come up with a way to extract one.

VALERIE. *(Laughing)* And you came up with this?

CHARLES. Not immediately. Henri gave me the idea. She told me how much you liked my books, how much you both enjoyed a good murder mystery. So I set about creating one for you.

VALERIE. Well, I must congratulate all of you. You gave marvellous performances.

McKENZIE. I should hope so. We've been rehearsing for months.

CHARLES. Yes, we had to be prepared for every eventuality. Even then, we weren't completely successful. Losing the journal certainly wasn't part of the plan. A pity it's gone. Apart from its value as evidence, it would have been worth a fortune.

VALERIE. Sorry about that.

CHARLES. And you caught us quite off guard when you suggested we burn the letters. However, Elwood came to our rescue at just the right time when he appeared with my letter pinned to his chest.

VALERIE. Good old Elwood.

*(ELWOOD rubs his chest and glares at WILLY.)*

CHARLES. I must say, you never gave anything away, Julia. We weren't expecting to have to play out the whole script before you finally cracked. Your stoicism is quite remarkable.

VALERIE. I've had a lot of practice. So tell me, how does this story of yours end?

CHARLES. Oh the story's over, Julia. Now we go home.

*(He puts cassette down on coffee table, pulls out a cell phone and begins to dial.)*

VALERIE. *(Taking in the phone.)* So everything about this weekend was pure fabrication.

WILLY. Well the storm wasn't our doing, but just about everything else was. The games every Halloween, the Bartleys, and all that stuff in the letters.

McKENZIE. *(Holding up the brandy bottle and the decanter.)* Even the booze was fake. You got the real thing, of course, but the rest of us were drinking cold tea. We had to keep our wits about us, after all.

CHARLES. Hello, Mortie? It's Charles. Can you call the police and ask them to come to Haddington House immediately? ... Right. We'll see you in a few minutes.

*(He disconnects, puts the phone on the coffee table and picks up the cassette tape.)*

VALERIE. If revenge is what you were after, why did you go to all this trouble? Why not just bring me here and shoot me?

CHARLES. We weren't interested in revenge. What we wanted was to bring you to justice. This whole weekend was created for the sole purpose of extracting a confession.

HENRI. In any case, we had already been to the police. They knew we were on to you. If you died suddenly, they would have come straight to us.

VALERIE. Of course. Much better to bring me here and scare the wits out of me. I assume the gun was just full of blanks?

CHARLES. That's right.

VALERIE. *(Crossing to fireplace, picking up a piece of the plate.)* So how did you get this plate to shatter on cue?

CHARLES. *(Following her.)* A small explosive on the back. Elwood set it off from the passageway.

VALERIE. How very clever.

*(Suddenly she wheels around and slices CHARLES in the neck with the piece of plate. Blood spurts. He howls and drops the cassette. VALERIE picks it up and grabs the poker. CHARLES is on his knees, moaning in agony.)*

McKENZIE. *(Starting to cross towards him.)* Charles! Are you okay?

HENRI. *(Taking a step.)* The tape!!!

VALERIE. Stay where you are! *(She brandishes the poker. McKENZIE and HENRI stop.)* Ah. What a pity. All those months of work to get my confession and now it's going up in flames – *(She tosses the cassette into the fire.)* just like all your other evidence.

ELWOOD. Damn you!

VALERIE. You're worse off now than you were before. Now you've got nothing.

McKENZIE. But we all heard you confess. We can testify!

VALERIE. Your testimony won't mean a thing without something to back it up. You were just too damn clever for your own good. You should have killed me when you had the chance.

ELWOOD. And go to jail for your murder? That's the last thing any of us would want.

*(WILLY suddenly lunges towards VALERIE. She takes a swing at him. He backs off. At that moment HENRI rushes at her, with a cry.)*

HENRI. NOOO!!!
VALERIE. Get away from me!

*(HENRI and VALERIE struggle. WILLY steps in to help.)*

HENRI. The tape, Willy, get the tape!

*(WILLY goes to the fire. Meanwhile, HENRI has managed to get hold of the poker. She backs away. VALERIE rushes at her and HENRI swings the poker, hitting her across the head. VALERIE falls to the floor, bleeding profusely. ELWOOD rushes over to her. A beat.)*

ELWOOD. My God, Henri, what have you done?

HENRI. *(Still clutching the poker.)* It was an accident.

CHARLES. Did you get the tape, Willy?

WILLY. No. It's gone.

McKENZIE. Where's that phone of yours, Charles? I think we're going to need an ambulance.

ELWOOD. It's too late for that, I'm afraid.

CHARLES. She's not dead. Please tell me she's not dead.

ELWOOD. I'm sorry.

*(The sound of a motorboat is heard coming closer. They all turn at the sound.)*

HENRI. Oh, my God. They're going to think it was murder.

*(They look at one another as the impact of the situation sinks in.)*

McKENZIE. What are we going to tell the police?

CHARLES. We'll tell them the truth.

HENRI. The truth? Who's going to believe that?

*(They all look to HENRI, then towards the window as the motorboat gets closer. Lights fade to black.)*

### END OF PLAY

## PROPERTIES

Fireplace
Portrait of Agatha Christie over fireplace
Bookcase with books, including one to open secret compartment
Window seat by large DSR window
Jack-o-Lantern with light in it on window seat (explodes)
Armchair
Footstool
Loveseat
Side table with lamp
Dinner table with 5 chairs
Crystal ball on table
Bowl of soup with spoon and napkin on table
Gun with lighter for flame
Cigar for Charles
Tape recorder taped under table
6 notepads
6 pencils
Little cards with instructions written on them (for Willy)
Cigar on mantelpiece (for Elwood)
Secret panel door
Plate of food covered with silver plate warmer (for Henri)
2-tiered drinks table with Brandy, other glass bottles and snifters
Humidor with cigars on mantelpiece
Wheelchair (for Willy)
Gun (for Elwood)
Curtains
Poker by fireplace (for Henri)
Small towel on drinks table (for Valerie)
3 letters in envelopes (for Valerie, Henri and Willy)
Sealed letter on drinks table (for Henri)
Dust-covered leather-bound manuscript (in secret compartment)
Flashlight (for McKenzie)
Lit candles
Sofa
Coffee table

Hatchet (buried in Elwood's chest)
Oil lamps
Letter pinned to Elwood's chest (for Charles)
Pile of letters
Charred remains of journal
Gun that cocks and fires (for Henri)
Old warn photo to burn (for Henri)
Plate on wall (gets shot at and smashes)
Towels to wipe off blood
Tape cassette (taken from recorder and tosses into fire)
Cell phone (for Charles)
Piece of plate to cut Charles' neck
Blood (for wounds and poker)

## COSTUMES

**HENRIETTE:**
Under-Underdress (for Henriette)
    Pink pajamas top
Underdress (for Henriette)
    Off white leggins
    Green dress with t-shirt dickey
    Green socks
    Brown boots
Overdress (for Madam O'Karma)
    Black with gold stars kaftan
    Gold belt
    Black and gold turban
    Red wig
    Glasses
QC - Remove
    Black with gold stars kaftan
    Gold belt
    Black and gold turban
    Red wig
    Glasses
    NO ADDITIONAL COSTUME PIECES
QC - Remove (USL on escape platform)
    Green dress with t-shirt dickey
    Green socks
    Brown boots
Add
    Pajamas bottoms
    Pink slippers
    Beige robe with flowers

**CHARLES:**
Underdress (for Charles)
    Collarless dress shirt
    Taupe pants
    Beige/brown stripe vest

Socks
Brown shoes
Overdress (for Dr. Konrad)
    Shirt and tie dickey
    Navy double breasted jacket
    Glasses
    Moustache
QC - Remove
    Shirt and tie dickey
    Navy double breasted jacket
    Glasses
    Moustache
Add
    Brown jacket (preset off stage, window seat)
QC - Remove
    Brown jacket
    Collarless dress shirt
    Taupe pants
    Beige/brown stripe vest
    Socks
    Brown shoes
Add
    Navy paisley pajamas
    Navy robe
    Slippers

## ELWOOD:

Underdress (for Elwood)
    Beige collarless shirt
    Black pants
    Socks
    Black shoes
Overdress (Father)
    Priest collar
    Black suit jacket
    Wig
    Moustache and beard

QC - Remove
    Priest collar
    Black suit jacket
    Wig
    Moustache and beard
Add
    Sweater for shoulders (preset on stage, window box)

**VALERIE:**
Underdress (for Valerie)
    Black sweater
    Black pants
    Black shoes
Overdress (for Mrs. McKnight)
    White apron
    White maid's cap
    White collar
    Glasses
QC - Remove
    White apron
    White maid's cap
    White collar
    Glasses
Add
    Brown suit jacket (preset on stage, SL arm of armchair)
QC - Remove (USR)
    Black sweater
    Black pants
    Black shoes
    Brown suit jacket
Add
    Black pokadot pajamas
    Black robe
    Silver slippers

**WILLY:**
Underdress (for Willy)
    White t-shirt

    Gold chain
    Jeans
    White socks
    Cowboy boots?
Overdress (for Ernie)
    Brown cardigan sweater
    Skull cap
QC - Remove
    Brown cardigan sweater
    Skull cap
Add
    Black suit jacket (preset on stage, window box)

## McKENZIE:
All USL
    Navy jacket and skirt
    Black shoes
    Wig
QC - Remove
    Navy jacket and skirt
    Wig
Add
    Red dress
    Red stole
QC - Remove
    Red dress
    Red stole
Add
    Black jumpsuit
    Animal print belt
QC - Remove
    Black jumpsuit
    Animal print belt
    Black shoes
Add
    Plaid robe
    White slippers

# ACT I / Scene 1

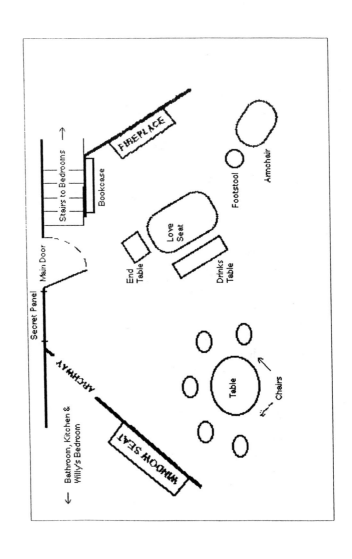

# ACT I / Scene 2
## and
## ACT II

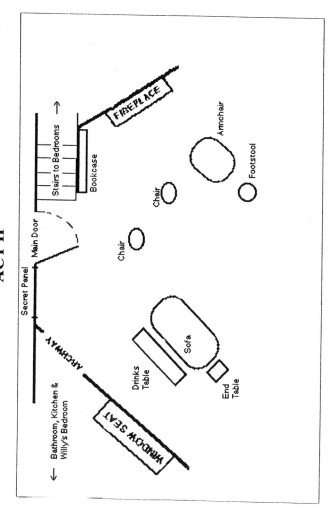

# New Thrillers from Samuel French, Inc.

ACCOMPLICE. (Little Theatre). Thriller. Rupert Holmes. 2m., 2f., plus one surprise guest star. Int. This truly unique new thriller by the author *The Mystery of Edwin Drood* broke all box office records at the Pasadena Playhouse, and went on to thrill audiences on Broadway. Sorry, but the only way we can describe the amazing plot for you is to "give it away." *Accomplice* starts out as a straightforward English thriller, set in a country house, in which a sex-starved wife plans, with the help of her lover, to murder her stuffy husband. All is, of course, not as it first seems. Oh, yes!— the "husband" is murdered onstage; but, later, he re-enters! Why? Because what we have actually been watching is a dress rehearsal. The play takes a new twist when we learn that this is an out-of-town tryout. The "husband" we have just seen "murdered" is actually the playwright and director of the play-within-the-play, and *he* has plotted to murder his *wife*, the actress playing the lead in his play, so that he can proceed unimpeded with his affair with her leading man. Got that so far? Well—you ain't seen *nothing* yet! A surprise character comes out of the audience (no—we won't tell you who it is), revealing that, in actuality, something entirely different is going on. A cast member is being set up—brilliantly and effectively, it turns out; and the cast has its final revenge against a fellow thespian whose cruelty resulted in the suicide of a friend. "The show is a delight. It is humorous, odd, scary, wildly dramatic, adult, adolescent— in short, impossible to dislike."—Pasadena Star-News. "Miss it at your peril."—L.A. Herald Examiner. "Wonderfully entertaining . . . a breathless ride through an ever-shifting series of planes."—Cleveland Plain Dealer. "A total delight."—Bergen News. "Part murder mystery, part sex farce and completely entertaining . . . suspenseful, charming and funny."—USA Today. Slightly restricted.                    (#3144)

MAKING A KILLING. (Little Theatre.) Thriller. John Nassivera. 2m., 2f. Comb. Int. A Broadway playwright, his conniving producer and his actress wife hatch a plot to guarantee their new play will be a success; they fake the suicide of the playwright on opening night! They then high-tail it up to Vermont where the playwright hopes to disappear, as he hates the public spotlight anyway. However, after a few weeks the playwright decides he no longer wants to participate in the scheme. Maybe his wife and his producer (who are having an affair) will have to kill him for real! Also on the scene is the playwright's feisty agent, who uncovers the plot and then helps her client deal with his most difficult artistic challenge: foiling his producer and wife! "A magnificent mystery thriller ... wonderful entertainment."—Bennington Banner. "Absorbing theatre."—Schenectady Gazette.                    (#15200)